Lily tried to move away but the arm that held her was tight, and in truth she didn't really want to move anywhere. She should just say no.

She should continue along on the perfectly reasonable theme of questioning his sobriety. She should tell him that her *primness* had been born out of a desperate need to protect herself from being hurt again. But wasn't the truth of it that none of these things seemed to matter in view of what he'd just said? That his unexpected proposal felt like a light which had been shone down onto the current darkness of her world.

"But why me?" she questioned shakily. "There must be a million women more suitable. Why ask *me?*"

"Actually, there aren't. There are very few women like you, Lily. I've certainly never met one before. And more than that—I have asked you because I can give you what you need."

What His Money Can't Buy

These powerful men have everything—except for the perfect wife!

Zac Constantinides and Ciro D'Angelo are among the richest men in the world. They share a passion for luxury, opulence and beauty.

So it's no wonder these international playboys strike a deal on London's premier hotel, The Granchester.

The only thing they have yet to acquire are suitable wives....

The polished beauties that usually adorn their arms are fine for the bedroom, but not the home. One thing is for sure, it will take a special kind of woman to tame these tycoons!

Watch the sparks fly in Sharon Kendrick's *fabulous* new duet:

Last month
PLAYING THE GREEK'S GAME
As Zac takes ownership of the hotel, he is shocked to find the Granchester's designer with her red-painted claws already in his brother! Emma is furious at her new boss's insinuations and just can't wait to take him down a peg or three!

This month
A TAINTED BEAUTY
As Ciro passes from the Granchester to his next acquisition, he's caught off guard by Lily's innocent beauty and is determined to have her as his wife. It's inconceivable that he could have gotten her so wrong, but now he's married there will be no turning back.

Sharon Kendrick

A TAINTED BEAUTY

HARLEQUIN®
entertain, enrich, inspire™

Recycling programs
for this product may
not exist in your area.

ISBN-13: 978-0-373-23858-3

A TAINTED BEAUTY

All about the author…
Sharon Kendrick

SHARON KENDRICK started storytelling at the age of eleven and has never really stopped. She likes to write fast-paced, feel-good romances with heroes who are so sexy they'll make your toes curl!

Born in west London, she now lives in the beautiful city of Winchester—where she can see the cathedral from her window (but only if she stands on tip-toe). She has two children, Celia and Patrick, and her passions include music, books, cooking and eating—and drifting off into wonderful daydreams while she works out new plots!

Visit Sharon at www.sharonkendrick.com.

Other titles by Sharon Kendrick available in eBook:

Harlequin Presents®

To the memory of the lovely Betty Boyer,
who helped make my English classes such fun
and who was always so bubbly.

CHAPTER ONE

Someone was watching her.

The little hairs prickled on the back of Lily's neck and somehow she just *knew*. Lifting her head from her pastry-making, she narrowed her eyes against the brightness outside to see the powerful figure of a man standing at the far end of the garden.

He was as still as a statue. Only his thick black hair seemed to move—ruffled by the same faint breeze which was drifting in through the open kitchen door as she worked. Unconsciously framed by a tumbling bower of early summer roses, he looked like a dark and indelible blot on the golden landscape and Lily's heart gave a funny little kick as he began walking towards the house.

For a moment she wondered why she didn't feel more scared. Why she wasn't screaming the place down and grabbing the nearest phone to tell the police that some dark stranger was lurking in the grounds. Maybe because the sight of him was a distraction from the troubled thoughts which kept nagging away at the corners of her mind. Or maybe there was just something about this particular stranger which overrode all normal considerations. He looked as if he had every right to be there. As if the soft summer day had been waiting just for him.

With a guilty kind of pleasure she watched the powerful thrust of his thighs against fine grey trousers as he walked across the manicured perfection of the emerald lawn. The light breeze was rippling the white shirt across his chest and defining the hard torso which lay beneath. *Poetry in motion*, thought Lily longingly—and could have watched him all day.

He grew closer and she could see the unashamed sensuality of his face. Thick-lashed dark eyes, which seemed to gleam with dangerous brilliance. A chiselled jaw, shadowed with virile new growth. And a pair of lips which she immediately began imagining imprinting themselves on hers. The kick in her heart became a full-scale football match as he stopped at the open doorway and Lily felt almost *dizzy*. How long had it been since she'd looked at a man and felt an overpowering sense of desire? And how could she have forgotten just how potent it could be?

'Can I...help you?' she questioned and then, realising how *passive* she sounded, she glared at him. 'You scared the life out of me—creeping up on me like that!'

'I wasn't aware that I was *creeping*,' he answered. His eyes met hers with a mocking look—as if he was perfectly aware that she had been drooling over him. 'But you look pretty capable of holding your own against any intruders.'

She realised that his gaze was now directed at her hand and that she was still holding her rolling pin, clutching onto it as if it were the latest thing in personal safety devices. Her tongue flicked out to moisten lips, which suddenly felt cracked and dry. 'I was just making pastry.'

'You don't say?' Ciro's amused glance took in the flour-covered table behind her:

the fruit-filled pie-dish and sugar shaker. And suddenly his senses were alerted by more than her soft beauty. The rare smell of home-baking in the cluttered room made him think of a world he'd only ever glimpsed. A world of warmth and cosy domesticity—and he felt an unexpected twist of his heart. But with habitual ruthlessness, he batted away his uncomfortable thoughts and looked at the pastry-maker instead.

She was the most old-fashioned woman he'd ever seen. The kind of female he didn't think existed any more—at least, not outside reruns of old TV shows. A tantalising composition of curves and beguiling shadows, she was wearing an apron—and he couldn't remember the last time he'd seen a woman wearing one of those. Not unless you counted the French maid outfit which his last-but-one lover used to wear in the bedroom, when she suspected he was tiring of her—which he was. That had been chosen to highlight the wearer's nakedness, but this was a much more innocent variation. A deliberately retro version in frilly cotton, it was tied tightly enough to emphasise the tiniest waist he'd ever seen.

Some people thought it was rude to stare—but when a man was confronted by a beautiful woman, wasn't it an insult not to? His eyes drifted to her thick hair, which was the colour of ripened corn and piled high on her head with a haphazard collection of clips. Her skin was flushed and he was amazed that a neck that slender could possibly support the weight of all that hair. He wondered if she realised what a perfect picture of domesticity she made. And he wondered what it said about him that he should find such an image so unexpectedly *sexy*.

'So aren't you going to invite me in?' he drawled.

The egotistical certainty of his question made Lily spring into action. Why was she standing there like some sort of muppet while he ran those admittedly gorgeous eyes over her as if she'd been some sort of car he was considering buying? Wasn't that why men thought they could get away with arrogant behaviour, because women like her let them? Hadn't she learnt *anything* from her past? 'No, I am not. For all I know, you could be an axe-murderer.'

'I can assure you that murder is the last thing on my mind,' he said drily.

Their eyes met and Lily heard the sudden roar of blood in her ears.

'And you don't look in the least bit scared,' he added silkily.

She swallowed down the lump which seemed to have taken up residence in her throat. It was true she wasn't exactly *frightened*. Well, not in the conventional sense. But there was something about him which was making her heart race in a way which wasn't a million miles away from fear. And the clamminess on the palms of her hands was going to play havoc with her pastry if she wasn't careful. 'It is normal to introduce yourself when you burst unannounced into someone's kitchen, you know,' she said primly.

He bit back a smile because even when women didn't know who he was, they were nearly always intimidated by him. But not this one, it seemed. Intrigued by the unfamiliar, he inclined his head as if they were being formally introduced at a social function. 'My name is Ciro D'Angelo.'

She stared into the dark gleam of his eyes. 'That's an unusual name.'

'I'm an unusual man.'

With difficulty, Lily decided to ignore the outrageous boast—mainly because she suspected it was true. 'And you're Italian?'

'Actually, I'm Neapolitan.' He gave a lazy shrug in answer to the question in her eyes. 'It's…different.'

'How?'

'That might take a long time to explain, *dolcezza.*'

The pounding in her heart increased especially when he said *dol-cezza* like that, though she didn't have a clue what it meant. She *wanted* to him to explain why Neapolitans were different but sensed that would be straying into even more dangerous waters. Instead, she deliberately glanced at the clock which hung next to the old-fashioned cooking range. 'Time which I don't have, I'm afraid,' she said crisply. 'And I'm still none the wiser. Just what are you doing here, Mr D'Angelo? This is private property, you know.'

Ciro gave an almost imperceptible nod of satisfaction because her question pleased him. It meant that news of his purchase hadn't been made public. Which was good. He hated publicity—but he particularly hated his deals getting into the public domain before the ink had dried on the paper. Despite his legendary prowess in the world of business, he was still superstitious enough to worry about jinxing things.

But her question also made him wonder who she was. The woman selling this house was middle-aged. He frowned as he racked his brains to remember the vendor's name. Scott, yes—that was it. Suzy Scott—all age-inappropriate clothes and too much make-up and a way of looking at a man which could only be described as hungry. He frowned. Was this domestic goddess old enough to be her daughter? he wondered, as he tried to work out just how old she actually was. Twenty-one? Twenty-two? With skin that clear and soft, it was hard to tell. And yet, if she *was* the daughter of the house—surely she would know it was about to pass into the ownership of someone else. *His* ownership, to be precise.

She was still looking at him questioningly and he noticed that a shiny tendril of corn-coloured hair was tickling the smooth surface of her cheek. Maybe he should just turn around and come back at a more legitimate time—but suddenly, Ciro didn't want to go anywhere. He felt as if he'd stumbled into a warm world which was so different from his own that he was curious to find out more. To discover its inevitable flaws so that he could walk away with his cynicism intact.

He gave a shrug of his powerful shoulders. 'I wasn't expecting to find anyone home.'

'You mean you have an expectation that all houses will be empty?' Aware that the pie would be ruined if she neglected it any longer, Lily curled the pastry around her rolling pin and then deftly flipped it over the top of the prepared pie-dish. 'What are you—some sort of cat burglar?'

'Do I look like a cat burglar?'

Glancing up from where her fingers were fluting the sides of the soft pastry, Lily thought not. She doubted that your average cat burglar would exhibit such a cool confidence if they'd been rumbled—though he certainly looked agile enough to accomplish the physical demands of the job. And it was frighteningly easy to imagine him clothed entirely in some sort of close-fitting black Lycra.

'You're not exactly dressed for it. I imagine that your expensive-looking suit might be ruined if you tried scaling the front of the house,' she said caustically. 'And in case you *were* thinking of scaling the front of this house—I can save you the time. You won't find any pr-precious jewels or baubles here.'

Viciously, she began to brush the pie crust with beaten egg, realising that she must be feeling especially vulnerable if she had just come out and told a complete stranger *that*. But Lily *had* been feeling vulnerable lately—and her stepmother's erratic behaviour hadn't helped. Never the easiest of women to get along with—Suzy had recently taken to moving the house's most valuable items up to her London home. Of course, she was perfectly within her rights to do so—Lily knew that. Suzy could do whatever she wanted since she had inherited every last bit of her late husband's estate. All the money he'd owned was now hers and so too was this beautiful house, the Grange.

Even now, the pain and injustice of it all could still hit Lily like a savage blow. Her father's death barely nine months after his second wedding had been sudden and unexpected and had left her with a numbing feeling of insecurity. Through her own grief and the heartbreaking task of comforting her younger brother, she had tried to tell herself that *of course* Dad must have been planning to amend his will. No father would want to see his two children left without any financial support, would he? But the fact was that he hadn't got around to doing it and it had all gone to his much younger wife, who seemed to have taken to widowhood alarmingly well.

Even the pearl necklace which Lily had been promised by her darling mother had been ferreted away to Suzy's metropolitan home and she had a sinking feeling she would never see it again. Was that why her stepmother had recently been shifting everything of value—afraid that Lily might pawn some of the precious artefacts when her back was turned? And the terrible thing was that an instant windfall *would* solve some of Lily's problems—because wouldn't it give her brother the security he deserved?

Ciro heard the tremble in her voice and wondered what had caused it. But his attention was distracted as she bent to place the pie in the oven, his eyes riveted to the seductive curve of her bottom. Her bare legs gave off a silky sheen and the little cotton dress she wore brushed close against her thighs.

'No, I'm not a cat burglar and I'm not after your jewels or your baubles,' he said unevenly.

Lily turned around to find his dark eyes fixed on her and, even though it was wrong, it felt good to have such a gorgeous man gazing at her with unashamed interest. Didn't it make her feel *desirable* for a change, instead of some invisible nobody who spent her whole time fighting off unspoken fears about the future?

'Then what are you doing here?'

'For some strange reason, it's gone clean out of my mind,' he said softly. 'I don't remember.'

Their gaze held and Lily didn't need the frantic bash of her heart against her ribcage to know they were flirting. It was a long time since she'd flirted with anyone and it felt...*dangerous*. Because the sensuality which was shimmering off his powerful body brought back too many memories and they weren't good ones. Memories of disbelief and heartbreak and a tear-soaked pillow.

'Well, *try*,' she said. 'Before I lose the little patience I have left.'

Ciro wondered what to tell her because it wasn't for *him* to enlighten her that he would soon be the owner of this house. But if she *worked* here...then wasn't it conceivable that he might keep her on once the sale went through? 'I've been looking for somewhere to buy,' he said.

Confused now, Lily stared at him. 'But this house isn't for sale.'

Ciro quashed a momentary feeling of guilt. 'I realise that,' he said truthfully. 'But you know how it is when you're scouting around an area—how you always notice the best things when you're not on a tight schedule? You see the sudden twist of a path, which makes you wonder where it leads. Yet the moment an agent starts detailing the square footage—you stop seeing a place for what it is, and it becomes simply real estate.'

'So you're saying you prowl around properties when you think they're empty—because they might appeal to you on an aesthetic level? No wonder I thought you were up to no good!'

But Ciro wasn't really listening. He found himself wanting to remove the pins from her hair so that he could see it tumble down over her shoulders. To splay his fingers over those fleshy hips and to dip his lips to the slender column of her neck and kiss it.

He told himself that he should leave right now and not return until the keys of the old house were in his hands. Yet the homeliness of the kitchen, combined with her old-fashioned body, was making him feel a sense of nostalgia which was sharpening his desire for her. Suddenly, it was all too easy to imagine what she might look like, naked—with all her curves and cushioned flesh. If he'd met her at a party, he would be well on the way towards making that fantasy a reality—but he'd never met a woman in a *kitchen* before.

'What can I smell?' he asked.

'You mean the cooking?'

'Well, you certainly haven't let me close enough to sample your perfume,' he drawled.

Lily swallowed, her skin prickling with nerves and excitement. 'There are several smells currently competing for your attention,' she said quickly. 'There is the soup bubbling away on the hob.'

'You mean home-made soup?'

'Well, it's certainly not out of a carton or a tin,' she said, with a shudder. 'It's spinach and lentil, lightly flavoured with coriander. Best served with a dollop of crème fraîche and a hunk of freshly baked bread.'

It sounded like an edible orgasm, Ciro thought irreverently and felt the heaving aching of his groin. 'Sounds delicious,' he said unevenly.

'I am reliably informed that it *is* delicious. While this—' she pointed towards a sticky-looking concoction which was sitting cooling on a rack '—is your common or garden lemon drizzle cake.'

'Wow,' he said softly.

She searched his face for signs of sarcasm but could find none and there was something about his almost *wistful* expression which made her throw caution to the wind. 'You could…try some, if you like. It tastes best when it's warm from the oven. Sit down and I'll cut you a slice. After all, if you've come all the way from Naples—the least I can do is show you a little English hospitality.'

Again, he heard the clamour of his conscience but Ciro blotted it out. Instead, he lowered himself into a solid-looking wooden chair and watched her as she moved around the kitchen. 'You still haven't told me your name.'

'You didn't ask.'

'I'm asking now.'

'It's Lily.'

His gaze travelled over her face and alighted on the soft curve of her lips. 'Pretty name.'

Hastily, she turned to take the milk-jug from the fridge, hating the fact that the meaningless compliment was making her blush. 'Thank you very much.'

'But I presume you have another name—or is that a state secret?'

'Very funny.' She met the glint of mischief in his eyes. 'It's Scott.'

'Scott?'

'As in great,' she explained automatically. 'You know, Great Scott—the explorer.'

'Yes, I know,' Ciro said, his mind spinning as he began to work out the implications. She *must* be related to the vendor. Yet how could that be when she didn't have a clue that the house had just been sold? When she didn't even realise that it had been on the market. He frowned, knowing that he had passed the point where he could decently tell her.

Except that wasn't quite true, was it? If she'd been middle-aged, or male and quite obviously a member of staff—he wouldn't have had any problem telling her that he was the new owner of this big house. It was her general gorgeousness which was making him hesitate about enlightening her. *And surely it wasn't his place to do so?*

He waited until she had poured tea and

he'd accepted a slice of delicious-looking cake for which he now had no appetite, before broaching the subject again. 'So you live here?'

Lily was so busy gazing dreamily at the shadowed slant of his chiselled jaw that she didn't really stop to think about his question.

'Of course I live here! Where did you think I…' And then she saw something in his eyes which made her voice change and she put down the cup which she had been about to raise to her lips. 'Oh, I see,' she said slowly. 'You thought I worked here? That I'm an employee. The cook, perhaps? Or maybe even the housekeeper.'

'I didn't—'

'Please don't feel you have to deny it—or to apologise.' She saw the uncomfortable look which had crossed his face and could have kicked herself. There she'd been— drifting around in some crazy dream-world, thinking that he actually fancied her when all the time he was looking on her as the hired help! Well done, Lily, she thought grimly. It seemed that her male radar was as unreliable as ever. She shook her head. 'I mean, of *course* someone like me wouldn't be living in a house like this. It's much too grand and expensive!'

He winced. 'I didn't say that.'

He didn't have to, thought Lily. And anyway, why deny something which was fundamentally true? She *did* make cakes for a living and she *did* dress on a budget—because that was pretty much all she had to live on these days. Didn't she squirrel away as much of her meagre wages as possible to send to her brother Jonny at boarding school—to stop him from standing out as the poor, scholarship boy he really was?

Yet maybe Ciro D'Angelo had done her a favour. Maybe it was time to recognise that nothing was the same any more. She needed to accept that things had moved on and she needed to move on with them. She was no longer the much-loved daughter of the house—because both her parents were dead. It was as simple as that. Her stepmother wasn't the evil stereotype beloved of fairy tales. She tolerated her, but she didn't love her. And since her father had died, Lily had increasingly got the feeling that she was nothing but an encumbrance.

She forced herself to say the words. To maintain her pride, even though she no longer had any legitimate position here. 'This is my stepmother's house,' she said. 'She isn't here at the moment, but she'll be back soon. In fact, very soon. So I think it's time you were leaving.'

Ciro rose to his feet, a hot sense of anger beginning to simmer inside him. Why the hell hadn't her stepmother told her that this house had been sold? That contracts had been exchanged and the deal would be completed within days. By the end of next week, the house would be his and he would begin the process of turning it from a rather neglected family home into a state-of-the-art boutique hotel. He frowned. And what was going to happen to this corn-haired beauty when that happened?

He made one last attempt to get her to stop glaring at him—to try to coax a smile from those beautiful lips or a brief crinkling of her bright blue eyes. He gave an exaggerated shrug of his shoulders, which women always found irresistible—particularly when it was accompanied by such a rueful expression. 'But I haven't eaten my cake yet.'

Lily steeled herself against the seductive gleam in his eyes—almost certain it was manipulative. What a poser he was—and how nearly she had been sucked in by his charm! 'Oh, I'm sure you'll get another opportunity to try some. There's a tea shop in the village which sells another just like it. You can buy some there any time you like,' she announced. 'And now, if you wouldn't mind excusing me—I've got a pie in the oven which needs my attention and I can't stand around chatting all day. Goodbye, Mr D'Angelo.'

She gestured towards the door, her smile nothing but a cool formality before she closed it firmly behind him—and Ciro found himself standing in the scented garden once more.

Frustratedly, he stared at the honeysuckle which was scrambling around the heavy oak door, because no woman had ever kicked him out before. Nor made him feel as if he would die if he didn't taste the petal softness of her lips. And no woman had ever looked at him as if she didn't care whether she never saw him again.

He swallowed as the powerful lust which engulfed him was replaced with a cocktail of feelings he didn't even want to begin to analyse.

Because he realised he hadn't thought of Eugenia.

Not once.

CHAPTER TWO

'I DON'T understand.' Feeling the blood drain from her face, Lily stared at her stepmother—as if waiting for her to turn round and tell her that was all some sort of sick joke.

'What's not to understand?' Suzy Scott stood beside the large, leaded windows of the drawing room—her expression registering no reaction to her stepdaughter's obvious distress. 'It's very simple, Lily. The house has been sold.'

Lily swallowed, shaking her head in denial. 'But you *can't* do that!' she whispered.

'Can't?' Suzy's perfectly plucked eyebrows were elevated into two symmetrical black curves. 'I'm afraid that I can. And I have. It's a fait accompli. The contracts have been signed, exchanged and completed. I'm sorry, Lily—but I really had no alternative.'

'But why? This house has been in my family for—'

'Yes, I know it has,' said Suzy tiredly. 'For hundreds of years. So your father always told me. But that doesn't really count for much in the cold, harsh light of day, does it? He didn't leave me with any form of pension, Lily—'

'He didn't know he was going to *die*!'

'And I really need the money,' Suzy continued, still without any change of expression. 'There's no regular income coming in and I need something to live off.'

Lily pursed her trembling lips together, willing herself not to burst into angry howls of rage. She wanted to suggest that her stepmother find some sort of job—but knew that would be as pointless as suggesting that she stop kitting herself out in top-to-toe designer clothes.

'But what about me?' she questioned. 'And more importantly—what about Jonny?'

Suzy's smile became tight. 'You're very welcome to stay over at my London house sometimes—you know you are. But you also know how cramped it is.'

Yes, Lily knew. But her thoughts and her fears were not for herself, but for her brother. Her darling brother who had already been through so much in his sixteen years. 'Jonny can't possibly live at the place in London,' she said, trying to imagine the gangling teenager let loose on all the ghastly spindly antiques which Suzy loved to keep in her metropolitan home.

Suzy fingered the diamond pendant which hung from a fine golden chain at her throat. 'There certainly isn't room for him and his enormous shoes littering up my sweet little mews house, that's for sure— which is why I've arranged for you to carry on living here.'

Lily blinked as a feeling of hope quelled her momentary terror. 'Here?' she echoed. 'You mean in the house?'

'No, not in the house,' said Suzy hastily. 'I can't see the new owner tolerating that! But I've had a word with Fiona Weston—'

'You've spoken to my boss?' asked Lily in confusion, because Fiona owned Crumpets!—the tearooms for which Lily had baked cakes and waitressed ever since she'd left school. Fiona was middle-aged and matronly and, to Lily's certain knowledge, she and her stepmother had never exchanged two words more meaningful than 'Happy Christmas'. 'To say what, exactly?'

Suzy shrugged. 'I explained the situation to her. I told her that I've been forced to sell the house and that it's left you with an accommodation problem—'

'That's one way of putting it, I suppose,' said Lily, trying to keep the bitterness from her voice.

'And she's perfectly willing to let you and Jonny have the flat above the tearoom—so you won't even have that far to go to work. It's been empty for ages—it's almost as if it's been waiting for you! So how's that for a solution?'

Lily stared at her stepmother, scarcely able to believe that she could come up with such an awful scenario and consider it a good idea. Yes, the flat had been empty for ages—but there was a good reason why. Nobody wanted to live right next door to the local pub—especially since it had undergone a refurbishment and acquired an all-day licence. The last royal wedding had inspired a feeling of 'community spirit'—which basically meant that there was now round-the-clock drinking by the locals—and a deafening din of noise, which carried on late into the night.

Lily couldn't think of anything worse than finishing one of her shifts and then making her way up the scruffy staircase to the two-roomed apartment above. Yet what choice did she have? She was hardly in a position to flounce off and make some kind of life for herself somewhere else. She had Jonny to think of. Jonny who relied on her to provide some kind of warm base. To give him the security he so desperately wanted and the home he really needed.

'So what do you think?' prompted Suzy.

Lily thought this was yet another example of how life could kick you in the teeth. But what was the point of saying words which would only fall on deaf ears? 'I'll go and see Fiona later,' she said.

'Good.'

Her head still spinning from the bomb-shell which had been dropped, Lily found herself wondering whether she would see much of Suzy after this—or whether her stepmother would want to cut ties completely. And wouldn't that be best, in the circumstances? Her father had been the glue which had held the precarious relationship together and now that he wasn't here any more... 'Why didn't you tell me, Suzy?' she questioned suddenly.

Suzy's manicured fingers nervously touched the diamond pendant once more. 'Tell you what?'

'That you'd decided to sell. If I'd known about it before, then maybe I could have mentally prepared myself. Worked out some different kind of fate for myself, rather than having it presented to me like this. Why spring it on me like this?'

Looking uncomfortable, Suzy wriggled her shoulders. 'That wasn't my doing. One of the conditions of sale was that I kept the identity of the buyer secret.'

'How bizarre. But presumably I'm allowed to know who it is now?'

'Well, not really.' Suzy's thumb moved rapidly over the glittering surface of the diamond. 'It's not for me to disclose anything.'

'Oh, for heaven's sake,' said Lily, her frayed nerves making her voice shake with unaccustomed anger. 'Is there really any reason…?' But her words tailed off as she heard the approaching throb of a powerful car and saw Suzy begin to swallow nervously. 'What is it?'

'He's here,' whispered her stepmother.

'Who's here?'

'The new *owner*.'

Lily heard a car stop and a door slam and then the crunch, crunch, crunch of heavy steps on the drive—and as the peal of the doorbell echoed through the large house some gut-deep instinct began to unsettle her. An instinct which was only compounded by the way that Suzy was touching her dark red hair—the unconscious gesture of a woman who knew that an attractive man was about to enter the room.

'Aren't you going to open it, Suzy?' she questioned, her voice miraculously steady even though her heart was racing so fast that she was surprised she didn't keel over.

'Yes, yes. Of course.'

Clattering away on her high heels, Suzy

went into the hallway and, through a kind of daze, Lily heard the opening of the front door and the sound of low voices. And one of them was a deep and accented voice… She wanted to scream. To put her hands over her eyes—to block out the now seemingly inevitable sight of Ciro D'Angelo walking into the room, her stepmother shadowing him like a bodyguard.

Lily wanted to feel anger—nothing but the pure, white heat of rage—but the worst thing was that her body seemed to have other ideas. Something he'd awoken in her the other day was clearly not going back to sleep. She felt the shimmering of awareness—as if every nerve-ending had become raw and exposed to his dark-eyed scrutiny. And far more dangerous was the urgent prickling of her breasts and the pooling of heat deep in her belly.

'Hello, Lily,' he said softly.

At this, Suzy stepped out of his shadow, her lips opening in bewilderment as she looked at each of them in turn. 'You mean you already know my step—er—you've met Lily before?'

'Yes, we've met,' said Lily, forcing herself to speak. To wrest back some of the control she felt had been sucked from her by the dark and sexy Neapolitan. He might have purchased her home and her stepmother might have just announced that she was being offered a crummy flat above a tearoom as a poor consolation prize, but she was damned if she'd let Ciro D'Angelo see the distress which was chewing her up inside. *And wasn't some of the distress caused by more than fear of the future? Wasn't it motivated by the desire she felt for him—which served as yet another illustration of her shocking lack of judgement when it came to men?*

She pursed her lips together to stop them from trembling and it was a moment before she felt composed enough to speak. 'Mr D'Angelo was lurking in the grounds the other day—in fact, he crept up on me and gave me quite a scare. But instead of doing the sensible thing and phoning the police to say that we had an intruder—I was stupid enough to let him in and listen to his ridiculous story. Something about being entranced by a beautiful twist in a path and wondering where it would lead.'

'I'm flattered you remember my words so accurately,' Ciro observed softly.

'Well, please don't be flattered, Mr D'Angelo—because that wasn't my intention,' Lily said, even though at the time she'd loved the poetry of his words. What an impressionable fool she had been. 'You were sneaking around—'

'Like a cat burglar?' he interjected silkily.

Digging her nails into the palms of her hands, Lily met the gleam of his eyes, his words reminding her of that brief intimacy they'd shared. When she'd flirted with the idea of him wearing black Lycra and he had flirted right back. When she'd felt light-headed with the sensation of being with an attractive man and her body had felt like a flower in the full heat of the sun. 'Like a thief,' she said fervently.

'Lily!' Suzy had now taken up a central position, as if she were the referee in a boxing ring. 'You really mustn't be so rude to Mr D'Angelo. He has made me an extremely generous offer for the Grange…an offer I couldn't possibly refuse.'

'I can be anything I please!' said Lily. '*I haven't been conducting secret deals with him!*'

'I'm so sorry about this.' Suzy turned to Ciro, curving her shiny lips into an exasperated smile. 'But I'm afraid that because we're so close in age, I've always had difficulty disciplining her—even when my late husband was alive.'

'Cl-close in age?' Lily spluttered indignantly.

Ciro saw that Lily's face was ashen and, overcome by a mixture of protectiveness and fury, he turned to the older woman. 'Mrs Scott, I wonder if you'd mind providing some refreshment? I've flown straight from New York and—'

'Of course. You must be exhausted—jet lag always completely lays me out, too!' gushed Suzy. 'Would you like coffee?'

'Coffee would be perfect,' he said coolly.

Suzy looked across the room at Lily and for a split second she thought her stepmother was about to ask *her* to make it, as she normally would have done if she'd had friends round. But something in her expression must have made her change her

mind because she merely gave her a quiz-
zical smile. 'Lily?'

'No, thanks. I think I need a real drink,'
said Lily, walking over to the drinks cabi-
net and yanking open the door, afraid that
if she didn't occupy herself with something
then she might just crumple to the carpet.
She was aware of Ciro's eyes burning into
her as she pulled out a crystal brandy glass
the size of a small goldfish bowl and reck-
lessly splashed in a large measure of the
most expensive brandy she could find.
Taking a large mouthful, she felt her eyes
water and she almost choked as the fiery
spirit burned her throat. But somehow she
managed to swallow it down and quickly
took another gulp to take the taste away.

'Easy,' warned Ciro.

She turned on him and the fear and insecurity she'd been suppressing now came
bubbling out in a bitter stream. 'Don't you
dare tell me to go "easy",' she breathed, because surely defiance and anger were pref-
erable to the hot tears which were stinging
at the backs of her eyes. 'I can't believe that
you sat down in my kitchen—sorry, *your*
kitchen—and gave me all that wistful stuff

about soup, when all the time…' She drew in a shuddering breath and felt the brandy fumes scorching through her nostrils. 'All the time, you must have been laughing at me, knowing that you were now the owner of this house while I had no idea.'

'I was not laughing at you,' he ground out.

'No? Then why didn't you do the decent thing and tell me you were the new owner?'

'I thought about it.' He paused and he could feel the tension in his body. A tension which had been there every time he'd thought about her. 'But it wasn't really my place to do so.'

'Why not?' She met his eyes—the brandy now burning in her stomach, giving her the courage to level an accusation she might normally have bitten back. 'Because you were too busy flirting with me?'

He shrugged. 'There was an element of that,' he conceded.

'So, what? You thought you'd see how far you could get before you came out and told me?'

'Lily!' he protested, taken aback by her burning sense of outrage. *And wasn't her re-*

sponse turning him on? For a man unused to any kind of resistance from a woman, wasn't it turning him on like crazy? 'I wasn't expecting to find anyone home—that much is true. And when I stumbled across you, well...'

His words tailed off because he was reluctant to explain himself. Admitting his feelings to women wasn't in his make-up— hadn't that been a complaint which was always being levelled against him? Eugenia had said it all the time, especially in those early days—when she had been trying to make herself into the kind of woman she thought he wanted.

Yet Ciro could never remember feeling quite so entranced by anyone as much as Lily Scott. She seemed to embody all the old-fashioned qualities he'd never found in a woman before—and hadn't her blue-eyed face and sexy body haunted him ever since?

'Well?' she demanded. 'You can't come up with a reasonable explanation, can you?'

Impatiently, he shook his head. 'If anyone should have told you, it was your stepmother.'

As if on cue, Suzy came back into the room carrying a tray with coffee and a plate of Lily's home-made ginger biscuits. Clearly she had overheard his last words because she put the tray down and gave him a reproachful look. 'That's not really fair, Ciro—since one of the conditions of your purchase was that I keep your identity secret.'

'My identity, yes,' he agreed, irritated by her over-familiarity, because he certainly couldn't remember telling her to call him by his Christian name. Or to keep batting her damned eyelashes at him like that. 'But I certainly didn't ask you to keep quiet about the actual sale. No wonder Lily is hurt and upset if she's just been told that in a few weeks' time she has nowhere to live.'

Suzy pouted. 'Oh, for heaven's sake! This isn't some Charles Dickens novel! She's not some homeless urchin, you know. I offered her space at my London place, but she turned her nose up at it.'

Lily had had enough. Feeling slightly nauseous now, she put the half-drunk glass of brandy down on a table. 'I'm not some

kind of *object* you can just move around!'
she declared.

'I don't like the thought of you being
thrown out of your home,' he said roughly,
thinking that she was now looking quite
alarmingly *fragile*. 'And I'm willing to help
in any way I can.'

She met his eyes, hating the way her
body prickled in response to their dark and
seeking gleam. 'Well, I neither want nor
need your help, Mr D'Angelo,' she said,
with as much dignity as was possible when
her head was spinning from the hastily
gulped brandy. With difficulty, she only
just stopped herself from swaying, but the
movement was enough to make Ciro move.

He stepped towards her, his hand instinctively reaching out to catch her wrist and
for a brief moment the rest of the world
seemed to fade away. Her skin seemed to
spark like a bonfire where he touched her
and all she was conscious of was him. *Him.*
Staring into the fathomless depths of his
dark eyes, her mouth as dry as flour as she
imagined him kissing her. Imagined him
pulling her into the powerful and protective
strength of his body and, to her horror, her

breasts began to tighten in response to her fantasy. 'Get…*off* me,' she croaked, wondering if he could feel the rapid thunder of her pulse and if he realised what was causing it. 'Just let me go.'

Reluctantly, he let her hand fall—his brow furrowing into a deep frown. 'Where are you going?' he demanded.

Lily glared at him. 'Not that it's any of your business,' she said, 'but I'm going to work.'

'You can't—'

'Can't? Oh, yes, I can! I can do anything I please,' she said, cutting across his words with fierce determination. 'I believe your sale is completing on the third of the month, is that right? So I'll make sure all my belongings will be out of here by then. Goodbye, Mr D'Angelo—and it really *is* goodbye this time.'

She could feel his gaze burning into her as she walked out of the room and somehow she made it up to the bedroom she'd had for as long as she could remember. It was only then, surrounded by the comfort of the familiar which would soon be gone, that Lily allowed the hot tears to fall.

CHAPTER THREE

'So what do you think, Lily? I know it's a bit small.'

Fiona Weston's soft voice penetrated Lily's thoughts as she stared out of the dusty apartment window onto the street below. The village wasn't exactly in a throbbing metropolis, but it still seemed unbelievably noisy when compared to the peace and quiet she was used to. A cluster of men were standing outside The Duchess of Cambridge pub, all clutching pints and puffing away at cigarettes. A man shot past on a scooter and Lily winced as it emitted a series of ear-splitting popping sounds.

Well, she was just going to have to get used to it. No more fragrant roses scenting the air outside her window—and no more gazing out at the distant woods or gently rolling fields. Instead, she was going to have to learn to live with the sound of people and cars—because the village car park was only a short distance away.

'It's…it's *lovely*, Fiona,' said Lily, with as much enthusiasm as she could muster, though it wasn't easy. The brandy she'd knocked back earlier had left her with a splitting headache and she couldn't get Ciro D'Angelo's dark face out of her mind. Or the memory of the way she'd responded when he'd caught hold of her wrist.

It was bad enough that his purchase had caused this dramatic turnaround in her fortunes, but it was made much worse by her reaction to him. He had made her feel vulnerable and he'd made her feel frustrated, too. And while a part of her had hated the rush of pleasure she'd felt when he'd touched her—hadn't the other part revelled in the feeling of sexual desire? She forced a smile. 'Absolutely lovely,' she repeated.

'Well, if you're sure,' said Fiona doubtfully. 'You can move in any time you want.'

Lily nodded like one of those old-fashioned dogs her grandfather used to have in the back of his car and she remembered his positive outlook on life. Shouldn't she be more like that? To start counting her blessings? 'I can't wait! It's such a fantastically *compact* little apartment—and with a lick of paint and a few pot-plants, you won't recognise the place.'

'It could certainly do with a facelift,' said Fiona. 'Though I don't know where your brother's going to sleep when he's home from school.'

Lily had been wondering the same thing herself. 'Oh, he's very adaptable,' she said, wondering if sixteen-year-old boys *ever* stopped growing. 'And I'm going to splash out and buy a lovely new sofa-bed,' she added.

'Good for you.' Fiona smiled. 'Anyway, I've kept the rent nice and low.'

She mentioned a sum which seemed outrageously modest. 'I can't possibly let you charge me something like that,' said Lily shakily.

'Oh, yes, you can,' said her boss, sounding quite fierce for once. 'You're a hard worker, Lily—and it's your cakes which keep the customers coming back for more.'

On an impulse, Lily reached out to hug the kindly woman who had given her flexible working hours since the village tea-rooms had opened. The undemanding job had provided refuge during the dark days of her mother's illness and her father's rapid remarriage. Hadn't it been a kind of release for Lily, to be able to lose herself in the simple routine of serving people cups of tea and slices of cake? And hadn't the reassuring routine helped numb the horrible reality of the district nurse arriving daily, to give Mum another pain-killing injection?

From working on Saturdays and during school holidays, Lily had gone full time at the age of eighteen and had never really looked back. She'd started as a waitress—and when Fiona had discovered that she had a gift for baking, she'd asked Lily to supply the cakes, which she'd done ever since. For a non-academic girl who needed to be there for her brother, the job had been a gift.

Turning away from the window, Lily smiled. 'Well, if that's all settled, I'd better get to work or we'll have some very discontented customers on our hands. And we can't have that.'

'No, we can't!' Fiona laughed as the two women went downstairs.

Pleased at having made a decision which seemed to be the only bright light on the horizon, Lily changed into her pink uniform and slipped on a pair of sensible shoes. But as she tidied her hair in front of the mirror she was horribly aware of the feverish glitter in her eyes and the two spots of colour which highlighted her pale cheeks.

She looked *different*.

Unsettled.

A little bit *wild*.

But it wasn't just shock at her changed circumstances which was responsible for her altered appearance. It was the reawakening of sexual desire, too, and she knew very well who was responsible for *that*.

The afternoon shift was hectic, but she was on duty with her friend Danielle, whom she'd known for ever. The tearoom's proximity to a church reputed to be the birthplace of a famous saint meant that there was always a steady stream of customers, but on a glorious sunny day like today the place was packed. The new ice-cream range was popular, they ran out of lemon drizzle cake—and Fiona had to drive to the cash-and-carry to stock up on strawberry jam. Yet Lily was grateful to be busy, because it stopped her from wondering just where her life was heading and what the future was going to be like now that the house had been sold.

Just before closing time, the last customer had wandered out and Danielle had disappeared to start the washing up, when the tinkling of a bell announced a new arrival. Stifling a sigh, which she quickly turned into a smile, Lily looked up from rearranging some cakes on a stand and looked straight into the dark eyes of Ciro D'Angelo.

Her smile froze to her lips as a shiver begin to skate over her skin. It didn't seem to matter that she was still angry with him—he seemed capable of creating a powerful reaction just by being in the same room. When he looked at her like that, she could feel the prickling of her skin in response.

'We close in ten minutes,' she said.

'I'll wait.'

Lily raised her eyebrows. 'Wait for what?'

'For you to finish.'

'Excuse me, but I think you might have mistaken me for somebody else.'

'I don't think you're easy to mistake for anyone else, Lily,' he said softly, making no attempt to hide the appreciative gaze which lingered on the luscious curve of her breasts. 'I've certainly never met anyone quite like you before.'

Angrily, Lily shook her head. There it was—another of those meaningless compliments which seemed to flow from his lips like honey. How many of those did he trot out on a daily basis, she wondered—and how many women ended up falling for them? She found herself lowering her voice, even though Danielle was well out of earshot and any sounds were drowned by the clatter of washing up. 'Didn't we just have a huge row?' she asked. 'And didn't I imply that I didn't want to see you again?'

Ciro shrugged. 'Things sometimes get said in the heat of the moment.'

'Things do—but I meant every word of them,' she insisted.

'Well, I'm here now—and the sign on the

door says you're still open,' he said, pulling out a chair and lowering his powerful frame into it. 'So I'm afraid you're going to have to serve me.'

Lily shot an anxious glance at the door— longing for Fiona to return and yet dreading it at the same time. She wanted him to go and yet she wanted to feast her eyes on him. In a place filled with paper doilies and flower-sprigged cake stands, he made the tearoom look completely unsubstantial. It was as if a giant had walked into a model village and taken up residence there.

'I want you to leave,' she said breathlessly.

His eyes sent her a mocking challenge. 'No, you don't.'

His silken taunt had an alarming effect on her and so did the sensual message which underpinned it and Lily could feel the distracting tightening of her breasts. She sucked in a deep breath. 'Obviously, I can't physically eject you.'

He elevated his dark brows. 'I agree you might have a little difficulty,' he murmured.

She glanced at her watch. 'We have exactly seven minutes until closing time—so I'd advise you to place your order quickly.'

'That's easy. I'd like some lemon cake—something like the one I missed out on last week.'

'I'm afraid we're right out of lemon cake.'

He gave a lazy smile. 'Is there anything else you recommend?'

'Well, since I make the cakes which are sold here, I'd recommend them all.'

Ciro's eyes narrowed. 'You do?'

'Yep.' She whipped out her order pad. 'And we've only got coffee or chocolate left—so which is it to be?'

'Scrub it.'

'Scrub what?'

'My order.'

He began to get up out of his chair and Lily felt her heart lurch with something which felt infuriatingly like disappointment. 'You've changed your mind?'

'*Sì, ho cambiato idea.* I have changed my mind.'

His sudden, seamless switch into Italian disorientated her, as did the fact that he had stepped up close to her—close enough to notice that dark rasp of new growth at his jaw which she had so wanted to touch before. And the stupid thing was that she still wanted to touch it. She wanted to touch *him*—to see whether he could possibly feel as good as he looked. 'What does that mean?' she questioned suspiciously.

'I'm agreeing with you. I don't want to sit here while you wait on me with that tight and angry look on your face,' he said.

'I'm glad you've taken the hint to leave me alone.'

'But I haven't.' He smiled with the confidence of a man who knew exactly what her response was going to be. 'Not until you've said you'll have dinner with me.'

Lily felt the crashing of her heart as those dark eyes bored into her. She could feel her cheeks growing hotter by the minute. He was so…so…*sure* of himself. 'Are you out of your mind?'

'I think I am a little, *sì*,' he said, unexpectedly. 'Because I haven't been able to stop thinking about you. I keep remembering the way you stood in that kitchen, with flour all over your hands and an apron around your tiny waist, looking like some old-fashioned domestic goddess. And believe me, it is not usual for me to be so pre-occupied with a woman.'

'I suppose it's usually the other way round, is it?' she observed sarcastically. 'Women completely obsessed by you from the moment they set eyes on you?'

'Can you blame them?' came his un-apologetic response accompanied by the faintest suggestion of a smile. 'But my undoubted appeal to the opposite sex isn't why I'm here today. I want you to know that I feel bad about what's happened.'

'At least there's *some* justice left in the world.'

Ciro bit back a smile. 'It was wrong of me not to have told you I was buying the Grange. But you must agree that I found myself in a difficult position.'

In spite of her determination to resist him, Lily found herself hesitating because surely that was genuine contrition she could read in his eyes? And it wasn't really his place to keep her up to speed on what was happening with the house, was it? 'Suzy should have told me sooner,' she conceded.

'Yes, she should.' Sensing capitulation,

Ciro smiled. 'So if there's no quarrel between us, then why not let me buy you dinner?'

She sucked in a deep breath. Maybe she should just be straight with him. Because Ciro D'Angelo was clearly a *player* and she didn't go in for casual sex with men—no matter how rich or how gorgeous they happened to be. 'I don't go out with men very often.'

'I find that very hard to believe.'

'Believe it, because it's true.'

'And I think you ought to make an exception in my case,' he murmured.

Lily stared into his dark eyes. His soft words were like fingertips whispering erotically over her skin. She should say no. Of course she should—because he was making her want to do things she didn't want to think about. Things she'd forgotten about. Or, rather, the person she'd forgotten about. The woman she'd been before her fiancé had dumped her. He made her want to wear silk stockings and tiny little scraps of barely there underwear. He made her want to feel his fingers tracking their way over her body and splaying against the cool flesh of her thigh. He made her feel things she'd forgotten she was capable of feeling—like pleasure and desire and a pure, raw yearning. And he might as well have had the word 'danger' stamped across his forehead in big red letters. 'I don't know,' she said.

Ciro smiled. He loved her hesitation. *Loved* it. 'Please.'

'And I'm just wondering,' she said slowly, 'why a cosmopolitan and obviously successful businessman like you is buying a big house in the middle of the English countryside.'

'You don't know?'

'How would I know, when it seems that I'm the last to know anything?'

There was a pause. 'I'm planning to turn it into a hotel.'

Lily's eyes widened. A *hotel*? 'You're going to turn the Grange into a hotel?' she breathed in horror.

'It will be a beautiful and tasteful hotel,' he defended. 'My hotels always are. Ask around if you don't believe me.'

But taste was subjective, wasn't it? Lily imagined the bedrooms turned from their faded familiarity into places with horrible swagged four-poster beds. She thought of corporate beige carpeting and those over-the-top hotel displays of flowers, which always made her think of funeral parlours. 'And that's supposed to reassure me?'

He felt like telling her that it was not her place to be reassured, yet he wanted her so much that he was prepared to overlook her impertinence. 'If it means that you'll have dinner with me, then, yes—be reassured. Come on, Lily. Just one evening. One dinner. What are you so frightened of?'

She wondered what he'd say if she answered 'everything'. If she told him that the whole world looked a terrifying place just now. That she was worrying about her brother's future. About how the two of them were going to adjust to living in that tiny apartment.

But hot on the trail of her fears came the realisation that she was becoming a bit of a hermit. She tried to remember the last time she'd been tempted to go out for dinner with a man. Her broken relationship with Tom had damaged her, yes—but wasn't she in danger of letting the damage deepen if she locked herself away, like some medieval woman in a tower? When had she last done something really reckless, just for the *hell* of it? Why *shouldn't* she spend the evening with Ciro D'Angelo—unless she really thought herself so spineless that she'd be unable to resist falling into bed with him?

'I don't want a late night,' she warned.

Ciro smiled as a feeling of triumph spread through his veins. 'What's your number?'

'407649,' she said, noticing that he didn't bother writing it down as he took a card from his pocket and handed it to her.

'I'll call you,' he said.

A figure appeared at the window— a middle-aged woman carrying jars of jam—and Ciro automatically got up to hold the door open for her, noticing her curious glance as she passed. Stepping outside into the sunlit day, his senses began to fizz with excitement. Because for a moment back then, he'd thought that Lily Scott was going to refuse to have dinner with him. A moment when he had tasted the unfamiliar flavour of uncertainty.

Yet wasn't this the way things were *supposed* to be, before emancipation had made women almost laughably easy? Before they'd mistakenly thought that behaving as predatorily as men was somehow a good thing. Men used to have to *work* at getting a woman into bed—this was just the first time in his life that it had ever happened to him.

He shot a last glance towards the tea-room, where he could see Lily's pink-covered curves in all their splendour and he could feel the powerful arrowing of lust. Was she aware that she had hooked him with a hunger which was tearing at his groin? His mouth flattened with a look which anyone who knew him would have recognised instantly. It was a look which preceded getting exactly what he wanted.

Because no matter how much she tried to resist him, Lily Scott would soon be in his bed.

She was, after all, only human.

CHAPTER FOUR

IT HAD been a *stupid* thing to agree to and Lily wondered what on earth had got into her. She should pick up the phone and tell Ciro D'Angelo she'd changed her mind. That she hadn't been thinking straight when she'd agreed to have dinner with him. But what could she possibly say to back that up, which wouldn't have her sounding like some kind of wimp?

I'm sorry, Ciro—but you make me feel all the things I've vowed never to feel again. You make me ache with longing when I look at you—and I don't do that stuff. Not any more.

But then it passed beyond the time when she could reasonably cancel—especially as her stepmother had come up to her room and started bombarding her with furious but unanswerable questions about why

Ciro D'Angelo had asked her out in the first place.

After she'd managed to get rid of her, Lily grabbed a quick shower—only just emerging dripping into a towel, when her brother rang from boarding school. Jonny loved the Grange even more than she did but he spent the entire conversation reassuring her that the new flat was going to be absolutely *fine* and that she wasn't to worry about a thing. She realised that at sixteen he was in for something of a shock when he saw their new home for himself. Yet there had been something about his determined bravery which had made her mouth wobble and she'd had to try very hard not to cry. He'd had so much to cope with in his short life, she thought fiercely—and this was just one more thing.

By the time she put down the phone it was getting on for eight and there wasn't time for much more than a lick of lipstick, or to pile the damp strands of her hair on top of her head in a rapid up-do. She hesitated over what to wear but ended up wriggling into a dress which was always guaranteed to lift her mood, no matter what. She'd made it herself from a vintage pattern in the feminine design of the fifties—the only style which seemed to suit her curvy figure. It was deep-blue and fitted, the sweetheart neckline a little on the low side, but the ankle brushing hemline made the dress feel relatively demure. And that was important on this particular night. She had no intention of giving out the wrong kind of message to Ciro D'Angelo. Of making him think that she would just fall into his arms as she was certain that every other woman did.

Hearing the sound of his car roaring down the drive soon after eight, Lily picked up her handbag, aware of the simmering waves of anger emanating from her stepmother who was standing by the front door like a guard-dog.

'Do you know what kind of man he is?' Suzy demanded.

'I'm sure you're going to tell me,' said Lily flatly.

'A billionaire who's famous the world over for his sophisticated conquests, that's who! A man who dates supermodels and heiresses! Care to tell me where you fit into that kind of world, Lily?' Running a speculative palm over a short skirt which made the very best of her undeniably good legs, Suzy adopted a look of sudden coyness. 'Why, he's closer to *my* age than yours.'

Lily opened the front door. Was he? She guessed he must be. What was he—mid-thirties? While Suzy was only just forty herself. A faint shiver ran through her as she looked at her beautiful stepmother and a disturbingly graphic image came to mind. Of Suzy coming on to Ciro and running those glossy red nails through the ebony gleam of his hair. Suddenly, she felt sick. 'What are you trying to say?'

'That he's out of your league!' With an effort, Suzy forced a smile. 'I'm only telling you for your own protection, Lily. I just don't want to see you get hurt.'

'Of course you don't,' said Lily quietly, closing the door behind her.

On suddenly shaky legs, she crunched her way over the gravel to where Ciro was just getting out of the car. And despite her reservations about her stepmother's motives, suddenly she could see exactly what Suzy had meant. Out of her league? Why, in his expensive suit, with his skin burnished gold by the evening sun, he looked like someone who'd fallen to earth from a different planet.

Yet he didn't resemble the seasoned seducer Suzy had just described. In fact, he was looking at her with a heart-stopping smile curving the edges of his incredible mouth.

'Dio, quanto sei incantevole,' he murmured as he held open the car door for her.

Lily slid onto the low seat. 'You do realise that not speaking Italian means I'm at a disadvantage, and I don't have a clue what that means?'

He hesitated for only a moment. 'It means that you look very...*nice.*'

Lily suspected that the word 'nice' wasn't one which featured in Ciro D'Angelo's vocabulary. And the look he was slanting at her certainly didn't make her feel 'nice'. In fact, it was making her feel deliciously and dangerously sexy. Demurely, she smoothed her dress down over her knees as he closed the door. 'Thanks.'

He got in beside her. 'I've left the roof

down—you don't mind? Women some-times fuss about their hair.'

Quashing down her faint feeling of hys-teria that already he was talking about other women, Lily shook her head. 'I've got so many pins in it that it would take a wind-tunnel to dislodge it.'

He shot her a curious glance. 'Do you never wear it down?'

'Not very often. It's so thick that it just gets in the way.'

'I'll bet it does.' Suddenly, he imagined what it might look like cascading over her bare breasts and an almost unbearable wave of desire washed over him. With an effort, he tried to think of something other than what kind of nipples she had. 'Have you decided where you're going to live?'

Lily gave a mirthless smile. He made it sound as if she had hundreds of choices at her fingertips. 'I'm going to be moving to the apartment above the teashop where I work.'

'And what's it like?'

She wondered how he would react if she answered 'like a shoebox'. 'Oh, it's very convenient for work,' she said stoically. 'It hasn't been lived in for a couple of years and it needs a little decorating. I want to make it look like home by the time Jonny arrives next week.'

Ciro's fingers tightened around the steering wheel as something unfamiliar exploded inside him. 'Jonny?'

'My brother.'

Her brother. If he'd suddenly heard that his share prices had just quadrupled in value, Ciro could not have felt more pleasure than he did at that moment. 'Your brother?'

'Yes. He's away at boarding school, but he'll be home next weekend. He hasn't seen the new place yet and I wanted to brighten it up for him.'

'How old is he?'

'Sixteen.'

'And you don't have any—'

'No, we don't have any parents.' Lily's words quickly cut through his as she anticipated the next question, because she'd heard it asked a million times before and always in that same slightly tentative tone which came pretty close to pity. 'They're both dead.'

'I'm sorry.'

'That's life.' She stared very hard at the road ahead. 'How about you?'

'My mother is still alive. She lives in Naples. My father…well, he died a long time ago.'

Lily heard the sudden bitterness which had entered his voice but the steeliness of his profile made her bite back the question which had been hovering on her lips. 'You see,' she said. 'Everybody has their own stuff which they carry around with them.'

'I guess they do,' said Ciro, finding himself in the unusual situation of having an intimate conversation with a woman he hadn't even had sex with. And the thought of having sex with her made him start to ache again.

'Why not just sit back and enjoy the ride?' he said unevenly.

Lily tried to do as he suggested, but it wasn't easy. She wanted to pretend that this was her life. She wanted to forget the cramped reality of her new home and the worry of how she could possibly make it feel big enough for Jonny, when he came home. And she wanted to stop feeling this powerful sexual attraction towards the dark and dangerous Neapolitan.

'Where are we going?' she asked.

'A place called The Meadow House—do you know it?'

'You mean the hotel?'

'That's the one,' he said, without missing a beat.

Lily gave her dress an unnecessary tug. 'You're staying there?'

'Mmm. I didn't want to drive back to London after dinner, and besides—' he glanced in his rear mirror '—I like to think of it as a bit of a fact-finding mission. Finding out what the local competition is like. They've just employed a Michelin-starred chef who's come from Paris to oversee the kitchen and I'm interested to know what's on the menu.'

Lily wasn't remotely interested in the food on offer, or the fortunes of some unknown chef, and she suspected that Ciro wasn't either. Because it didn't matter how he dressed it up. The bottom line was that he was taking her back to his hotel—and the message from that was loud and clear. He obviously expected her to sleep with him!

She glanced down at his powerful thighs. At the strong, olive-skinned hands which bit into the soft leather of the steering wheel as if it were a woman's flesh. *Of course he expected her to sleep with him!* He was a red-blooded Italian man and the atmosphere between them had been sizzling from the get-go. He was hardly bringing her to his hotel for an evening of sophisticated chit-chat!

But she was disappointed that he could be so...*obvious.* Despite all her reservations about this date, she'd expected him to at least have a *stab* at playing the gentleman. Did he really think she was going to fall into bed with him simply because she'd agreed to have dinner? She stared at the hedgerows which were whipping past them, their leaves gilded rose-gold by the light of the setting sun. Because if that was the case—then he was in for a shock.

Lost in thought, Lily barely noticed the rest of the journey until the car slid to a halt in the car park at the back of The Meadow House, alongside a fleet of other shiny and expensive vehicles. She followed Ciro into the main reception where everyone seemed to know him, and they were taken through to the garden at the back.

Here, the tables had been laid up as if the management had suddenly decided to hold an impromptu picnic. The place settings had a Bohemian look, with mismatched crockery and wine glasses which were coloured ruby, emerald and amber. Starry jasmine scented the air and tea-lights glimmered on every available surface, so that it felt like walking into an intimate arena of flickering light.

Despite her reservations about the evening ahead, or the fact that their arrival had attracted the interest of the upmarket diners, Lily was enchanted as she looked around. 'Oh, it's beautiful,' she said softly.

Ciro watched as the candlelight gilded her golden head. 'You've never been here before?'

'Never.'

He heard the trace of wistfulness in her voice as they sat down and once again he found himself wondering why she sometimes seemed so *lost*. As if she'd suddenly found herself alone in a great big world with most of the cares of it on her slender shoulders. *What had happened to make her like that?* He waited until they'd ordered and their champagne had been poured, before sitting back and studying her.

The candlelight was casting flickering shadows over the pale skin of her décolletage, deepening the shadows where her luscious breasts curved invitingly.

'Pretty dress,' he murmured.

'Really?'

'Really. Pretty colour, too. Did you buy it especially to match your eyes?'

Lily smiled. She'd bought the material because it had been in the end-of-line bin and an absolute bargain. 'Actually, I didn't buy it at all. I made it myself.'

'You make your own clothes?'

If she'd announced that she wing-walked on light aircraft, he couldn't have looked or sounded more shocked. 'You seem surprised.'

'That's because I am.' Ciro took a sip of water to ease the sudden dryness in his throat. 'I don't usually come across women who are quite so accomplished, or so hard-working.'

'No?' Lily couldn't stop herself. 'Then

what kind of women *do* you usually come across?'

There was a pause as Ciro considered her question. He thought of pencil skirts and killer stilettos. Of glossy lips and crotchless panties. Of women who were this soft, sweet creature's very antithesis. He thought of Eugenia, with her impeccable pedigree and beautiful, calculating expression. And he looked into Lily's blue eyes and nobody seemed to exist in that moment except for her. 'Nobody who matters,' he said softly. 'And here comes our food.'

The waiter brought plates of squash, fanned into artistic golden slivers and dotted with soft goat's cheese, and Lily stared at it, wondering if she would be able to do it justice. How ironic to be presented with such delicious food on the one time her normally robust appetite seemed to have deserted her. But maybe Ciro felt the same way, judging from the way he was picking uninterestedly at his starter.

Their barely touched plates were replaced with fish and vegetables and Lily forced herself to eat some more, looking up to find his dark eyes fixed intently on her as she finished a mouthful.

'I have spinach in my teeth?' she said.

He shook his head, envying any vegetable which had been given such intimate access. 'Your teeth are perfect. I'm just curious about you, that's all.'

She pushed her plate away and picked up her wine glass. 'In what way?'

'I want to know why you're leaving the Grange to share a flat above a tearoom with your brother.'

'Because my father didn't make a will.'

'Why not?'

Lily's fingers tightened around the stem of her wine glass, his words reminding her of all the upheaval which lay ahead. 'Because he remarried after my mother died—to a woman much younger than him. And presumably he was too…well, too preoccupied to remember to keep his affairs up to date. Not that there was much time for that.' She worried her teeth along the surface of her lip, almost glad of that brief moment of discomfort. 'They'd only been married ten months when he dropped dead from a heart attack.'

'I'm sorry,' he said simply.

The sympathy in his voice took Lily back to a memory she'd tried her best to erase—but some memories were too big and dramatic to ever forget. The image of her father clutching at his chest—his face waxy and beaded with sweat. The piercing sound of her stepmother's hysterical screams echoing around the dining room. After shouting at Suzy to call the ambulance, Lily had done what she could—but it had been in vain. A first-aid certificate was pretty useless when it came to single-handedly trying to resuscitate a middle-aged man who was considerably overweight—and Tony Scott had been pronounced dead at the scene.

Quickly, Lily raised her champagne glass to her lips and took a deep mouthful, the sharp bubbles making her blink. 'Stuff happens,' she said, in a flat voice. 'You can't change it. Suzy got everything and I had to accept that.'

Ciro's eyes narrowed. She showed a remarkable lack of resentment about her fate, he thought—especially as her stepmother seemed to have no qualms about sending her out penniless into the world.

'So you don't have an income?'

'Actually, I do,' she said defensively. 'It might not be quite in your league, but I make money from my cake-making and my waitressing, just in case you'd forgotten.'

Ciro bit back his instinctive response—that what she earned was little more than pocket money. 'It's admirable to find a woman who works so hard,' he said truthfully.

'Anyway,' she continued, brushing aside his unexpected compliment with the air of someone determined to change the subject, 'that's enough about me. You're the man of mystery—and so far I know very little about you.'

'I'm surprised you haven't looked me up.'

'And where would I do that?'

'On the Net.'

She stared at him curiously. 'Is that what people usually do?'

'It happens all the time.' He shrugged. 'Information is so easy to obtain these days—the only trouble is that not all of it is accurate.'

She heard the cynicism in his voice and thought that must be one of the drawbacks to being powerful—that people would always be interested in you. That they'd always know more about you than you did about them. Always have an agenda, too, she guessed. 'Anyway, I don't even have a computer.'

'Now that,' he said, a smile curving the edges of his lips, 'I do not believe.'

'It's true! I've always been more of a doer, than a reader. And why would I want to waste my time looking at a screen and spending hours on all that social media stuff, when there are so many lovely things I could be looking at in the real world?'

He started laughing, the sound causing a silent couple at a nearby table to glance over at them with unconcealed envy. 'Are you for real, Lily Scott?' he questioned softly.

Lily felt disorientated. That soft, dark look he was giving her was making her feel weak. More than weak. It was making her feel *vulnerable*. And tense. Beneath the soft material of her blue dress she could feel the insistent tug of her nipples and the soft pooling of desire deep in her belly. *This is dangerous*, she thought.

'Yes, I'm real enough,' she said. 'But so far, you're not. What should I know about you before you bring in your fleet of bull-dozers?'

'There seems to be a misconception about developers,' he countered. 'That they do nothing but destroy.'

'What, when really they're just sweet environmentalists who are planning to encourage swarms of butterflies into the area?'

'I'm not planning to raze the house to the ground, Lily.'

'Really?'

He looked straight into her eyes. 'Really,' he affirmed softly. 'I'm planning a con-version in keeping with the building, if you must know. I'll restore your beautiful house to its former splendour and turn it into a hotel. The kind of hotel where peo-ple will pay a premium for quiet and laid-back luxury.'

Lily stared at him. It didn't exactly fill

her with joy to think of her old home being available for hire in the future. To imagine people renting out the room in which she'd been born. But maybe if it had to be sold to a hotelier, then Ciro D'Angelo might just be the best kind. Just imagine if he'd been planning to put an ugly housing development there, or had wanted to erect some horrible modern monstrosity in its place. 'I suppose that doesn't sound *too* bad,' she said cautiously.

'I'm glad that my scheme meets with your approval,' he said gravely.

'I wouldn't go quite that far—and you've still managed to avoid telling me anything about yourself.'

'What exactly do you want to know, *dolcezza*?'

She wanted to know what it would be like to feel his lips pressing down hard on hers. 'Do you have brothers?'

'No.'

Or how it would feel to be crushed against that hard and virile body. 'Sisters?'

He shook his head. 'No.'

With an effort, she pushed away her wayward thoughts. 'And was it a...*happy* childhood?'

His eyes narrowed. Should he come right out and tell her the truth? That in its way, it had been a particular type of hell. He remembered lying in the silent darkness, listening for the first sound of his mother's high-heeled shoes hitting the marble steps. Holding his breath to discover whether or not she was alone or whether he would hear the murmur of male laughter and her own muffled response. He gave the hint of a shrug. 'It was okay.'

She wondered what had made his dark eyes grow so stony. 'Just okay?' she questioned.

A cool expression iced the dark angles of his face. 'Is this supposed to be a dinner date, or a therapy session?'

Through the flickering light of the candles she could see the tightening of his mouth and suddenly Lily didn't want to spoil the evening. 'I didn't mean to pry,' she said quietly.

But somehow Ciro knew that. Had he been unnecessarily harsh with her, when it had been concern and not curiosity which he could hear in her voice? 'You're talking about something which happened a long time ago,' he said. 'Something I prefer not to dwell on. At heart, all you need to know about me is that I'm just a simple boy from Naples.'

His expression was so irresistible, his assertion so completely outrageous that Lily started laughing. 'Of course you are.'

He leaned forward. 'Who badly wants to kiss the woman sitting opposite him.'

Lily put down her glass, afraid that the sudden trembling of her hand would cause it to topple. 'Stop it,' she whispered.

'Why? Is it so wrong to say what we've both been thinking all night?'

'You haven't got a clue what I'm thinking, Ciro.'

'Oh, I think I have a pretty good idea. I've been watching you very carefully and you cannot disguise the look in your eyes or the reaction of your body. I know you want me, Lily, just as I want you—and only a fool would deny that. I think I've wanted you ever since I saw you making pastry, wearing that cute, flowery little apron.'

Lily stared at him, her heart pounding.

He was looking at her with an expression which was making her tingle with a delicious heat. Her skin felt as if it were too tight for her body—as if every pore of it were stretched like a drum—and suddenly she was scared. Her stepmother might have been motivated by self-interest, but everything she'd said about Ciro had been true, hadn't it? He dated models and actresses. He was wealthy and powerful. He came from a different world.

She smiled. The kind of smile she'd have given anyone if they'd just bought her a delicious supper. 'It's been a long day,' she said. 'And I'm pretty tired. I think I'd like to go home now.'

'Sure,' he answered, non-committally—not at all perturbed by her deliberate change of subject. He saw her relax as they both got to their feet but he didn't feel one pang of guilt as he uttered the words he didn't mean. Because he wasn't planning to keep her here by *force*, was he? To take her upstairs to his suite and chain her to the huge bed. He was planning to kiss her, that was all. And after that, all her resistance would simply melt away—it was as inevitable as the rising of the moon which was gleaming silver in the sky above them.

This time, he didn't take her through the hotel reception on their way to the car, but pointed to a way which was heavy with the scent of newly mown grass.

'Where are we going?' asked Lily apprehensively as they stepped away from the lighted area around the tables.

'I thought that a woman who enjoys looking at the real world would enjoy a more scenic stroll to the car park, than walking through a busy reception area.'

Afterwards, of course, she berated herself for not having insisted on the more traditional route, but the illuminated trees he was gesturing towards looked too beautiful to resist. And the winding path was cleverly lit to make Lily feel as if she'd fallen into some magical woodland. Silvery light illuminated the smooth trunks of the beech trees and tall grasses waved their feathery golden fronds. If it had been any other time and with any other person, she might have taken more pleasure in the surreal beauty which surrounded her.

But as they walked along she found that

she could scarcely breathe… She was so *aware* of him. Every single part of him. Her nerve-endings seemed to be screaming out to have him touch her. To follow up the unashamedly erotic promise of his words with his hands and his mouth.

She'd never been so glad—nor so sad—to see his gleaming sports car and as he bent to put his key in the lock of the passenger door he suddenly halted—as if someone had just told him to freeze.

'Lily,' he said softly.

Just that. Maybe if he'd said something clever or flirtatious, then she would have been left feeling cold. As it was, she just stared into his eyes, their darkness fathoms deep—and she was lost.

And Ciro D'Angelo must have instinctively known that because he made a throaty little murmur as he pulled her into his arms and began to kiss her.

CHAPTER FIVE

IT WAS a kiss like no other and it reeled Lily straight in. The first brush of Ciro's lips against hers set off a sizzling reaction, which instantly made her want more. At first he teased her with the lightest of kisses and then he deepened it, provocatively licking his tongue inside her mouth—and it felt such a wickedly intimate penetration that her knees sagged.

Maybe that was the signal he'd been waiting for. The one which made him catch her by the waist while his other hand reached up to cushion her head, still kissing her with a thoroughness which took her breath away. She could feel his fingers impatiently weaving their way into her hair as he pushed her back up against the car. Suddenly, she was trapped, with no place to go—but surely this was a trap that no woman would want to escape?

Against her back was the coolness of the car and at her front was one hot and very aroused man. Her palms were splayed out over the smooth metal, she could feel the weight of his body pressing hard against hers—but not as hard as she wanted him. There was the sense that he was on fire, but was somehow managing to hold it back. As if he was deliberately banking up the flames of desire so that they smouldered away intensely.

And Lily couldn't stop herself from responding. It had been a long time since she'd been kissed—and she realised that there was no feeling in the world like this. She'd forgotten that passion could swamp you with its powerful sweetness. Could make the rest of the world recede until it seemed completely inconsequential. His kiss made her troubles fade away until it was only her and him and a hunger which was building and building—making her body shake with longing.

She opened her mouth wider to give him

better access and he moaned in response as if she had just done something very clever. *I shouldn't be doing this*, she found herself thinking as his hand moved away from her hair to cup one aching breast. *And I definitely shouldn't be doing it with him.* It took every bit of resolve she possessed, but somehow she tore her lips away from his and stared dazedly into his face.

Struggling to recover his breath, Ciro raked his gaze over her, taking in her darkened eyes and parted lips. The swollen thrust of her breasts strained towards him invitingly. He knew he should take her inside before things happened. Before they got so carried away that it would be as much as he could do to stop from unzipping himself and slipping aside her panties and just doing it to her there, right up against the side of the car.

He moved his hand inside the bodice of her dress where he could feel the peak of her hardened nipple against her bra and had to close his eyes briefly, seriously afraid that he might come there and then.

'Let us go up to my suite,' he said urgently as he drew his thumb over the sensitised nub and felt her shiver in response. 'Before someone comes out and finds us and we get arrested for public indecency.'

The breath had caught in Lily's throat and she felt as if someone were trying to tear her in two. On the one hand she had the sensation of Ciro playing with her swollen breast and the correspondingly acute shafts of pleasure which were shooting through her. While on the other...

She swallowed.

He was pressing his erection flagrantly against her belly! He was talking in a low and insistent voice about taking her up to his suite. And what would that involve? A dishevelled journey past the knowing eyes of the hotel staff, followed by a terrible walk of shame in the morning. What did she think she was *doing*?

With an effort she peeled her clammy palms away from the car and pushed them up against the solid wall of his chest.

'I think you forget yourself,' she said fiercely.

Ciro's eyes narrowed and for a moment

he thought she was joking—because surely she wasn't pushing him away after the chemistry which had just combusted between them? But then he saw the mulish expression which had tightened her lips and it dawned on him that she might actually mean it.

'You don't want to make love with me?' he questioned, his accent sounding far more pronounced than usual.

'Make *love*?' she snapped. 'Is that how you describe doing it out of doors, up against a car?'

He thought her accusation a little unjust, considering that she had been a very willing participant—but his indignation was quickly replaced by another wave of lust. And suddenly he didn't want her angry, with those darkened eyes spitting indignation at him. He wanted her soft and gentle again. He wanted to take her up to his suite and undress her very slowly. To lay her down on the bed and explore her body with his eyes and his hands and his mouth. He wanted to spread wide her beautiful thighs and slowly ease himself into her tight and waiting heat.

'It is true that we got a little carried away,' he said unevenly.

Lily shook her head, unable to believe that she'd behaved so badly—and after everything she'd vowed, too.

'I th-think that's something of an understatement,' she said shakily, repositioning the pins in her hair with trembling fingers. 'Now will you take me home, Ciro? Because if you won't, then I shall just walk inside and order myself a cab.'

Ciro frowned with frustration tempered by a feeling of awe. Didn't she realise that she was turning down a man reputed to be one of the best lovers in Italy? He thought about all the women who came onto him and shook his head in slight bemusement. It seemed that Lily Scott's behaviour really did match her prim appearance—and that she had a steely morality about her.

'Of course I will take you home,' he said, pulling open the car door and meeting the look of suspicion which had narrowed her eyes. 'Oh, please don't worry,' he added acidly. 'I am not so desperate for a woman that I will leap on her after she has said no.'

Lily nodded, grateful she wasn't going to have to hang around for a taxi—because what on earth would the hotel reception staff think?

'Thank you,' she said stiffly as she got into the car, wishing she didn't *care* what other people thought—but the truth was, she did. Maybe it was a consequence of having been jilted and those awful days when she'd been at rock-bottom and not sure who knew that Tom had gone and who didn't. When she'd thought that people were talking about her behind her back and judging her. Wondering what was so wrong with her that a man could just walk away and marry somebody else. That rejection had deeply affected her behaviour; it still did. Clipping shut her seat belt, she stared ahead.

Climbing into the driver's seat beside her, Ciro closed the roof of the car, his mind spinning. Suddenly he felt at a loss—he, who was never at a loss. There'd never been a situation with a woman which he didn't know how to handle—except maybe for the time he'd lost his virginity, aged fifteen.

Actually, even on the night he had bade farewell to his innocence, he'd taken to sex like a duck to water. Hadn't his thirty-year-old lover lain satiated on the bed afterwards, stroking his balls and telling him that he was going to make a lot of women very happy?

The crude progression of his thoughts did little to sate his sexual hunger but it did have the effect of bringing him to his senses. Wasn't it a terrible reflection of the life he lived, that he was shocked when a woman actually behaved like a *lady* for once? And didn't part of him actually *admire* Lily's stern rejection of his sexual advances?

He glanced at her, seeing the stony set of her profile as she stared fixedly ahead of her. 'I have a feeling that you might be expecting some sort of apology for what just happened.'

'It was a regrettable mistake,' she said calmly. 'That's all.'

Ciro clutched the soft leather of the steering wheel, scarcely able to believe his ears, and if he hadn't been so frustrated he might almost have laughed aloud. A *regrettable mistake*? Was she *serious*? Judging by the look on her face, it seemed as if she was. And wasn't that a little hypocritical? Why, she'd hardly behaved like the Madonna herself, had she?

'And are you always such an enthusiastic participant when making "regrettable mistakes"?' he questioned coolly.

'Perhaps I was led astray by someone with considerably more experience than me.'

Doubtless, she had meant the remark to be a criticism, but Ciro found himself giving a nod of satisfaction as he realised its implications. Of *course* he was more experienced than she was! Only an innocent or a very experienced woman would have behaved with such heart-stopping passion and then acted outraged—and she certainly wasn't the latter.

His thoughts began to race—and in a previously unexplored direction. He had found the evening surprisingly enjoyable, apart from its frustrating conclusion. He had actually enjoyed talking to her. She wanted to take it slowly—well, what was wrong with that? Wasn't that the way that people always *used* to behave, before the women's movement and freely available contraception led to the expectation of instant gratification?

Imagine what it would be like to actually have to *wait* for a woman to go to bed with you. To have to quash the urgent tide of sexual desire which was swelling up inside you. Mightn't that produce the most sensational love-making of all?

His car swung into the long gravel drive which led to the Grange and he sensed her tension as she looked up towards the upstairs windows, where a light was still on. Was the greedy stepmother still up and waiting for her? he wondered. And if that was the case, then maybe it was best that he *had* brought her home. Not good for either of their reputations if he'd brought her back tomorrow morning, still wearing the same dress...

'Stop just here, will you?' said Lily quickly.

She had already unclipped her seat belt and was reaching for the door-handle. 'Don't worry, I'm not going to bite,' he said wryly.

Lily thought how ironic it was that he should have said that, when not so long ago she'd wanted him to graze his teeth all over her aching nipple. 'Thank you very much for the dinner,' she said formally. 'I enjoyed it very much.'

He gave a low laugh. She really *was* a one-off. She sounded so *uptight*. But despite his intense frustration, he felt an unfamiliar sense of exultance, too—because the novelty of this situation was exhilarating. How many times had a woman said 'no' to him and meant it—even though the chemistry between them had been sizzlingly hot? Never. It had never happened to him before. He saw a woman, he wanted her and then he bedded her—it was as simple as that. Except this time. This time it had been nothing like that. 'So when am I going to see you again?'

There was a split-second pause before Lily turned to face him, steeling herself against his dark beauty and knowing that she'd be crazy to put herself in a similar position again. To open herself up to a vulnerability which she knew to be dangerous and to run the risk of being rejected again. She'd managed to hold him off because some shred of decency had arrived in time to stop her making a fool of herself, but she couldn't guarantee being strong enough to resist him next time. Especially not if he used that abundance of Neapolitan charm to whittle away at her already weakened defences. When even now she was having to fight the urge to throw herself into his arms and lose herself in the fleeting passion of his kiss. 'You're not,' she said quietly.

Ciro's dark brows rose in disbelief. 'Excuse me?'

She licked her dry lips. 'You're not going to see me again.'

'Why not?'

'Because I don't really think I'm your kind of woman.'

Night-dark eyes pierced her with their ebony gleam. 'And don't you think I ought to be the judge of that?'

'No,' she said fervently, telling herself that she mustn't let his persuasiveness influence what she knew to be the right decision. 'I don't. Because I don't think you're thinking straight—not at the moment, anyway. We…we live in different worlds, Ciro—you know we do. You're an international hotelier from Naples and I'm…well, I'm a small-town girl who bakes cakes and waitresses for a living. Perhaps we'll run into each other once you start work on making the house into an…' she gulped down a lungful of air '…hotel. But if we do, then it's probably best if we just smile politely at each other and go on our separate ways.'

Ciro shook his head. *Smile politely? Go their separate ways?* Did she have no idea about the kind of man he was? As if he would ever smile politely at a woman he was planning to take as his next lover. His masculinity had never been outraged—but, to his surprise, it was not anger he felt as a result, but a fierce sense of destiny. And of challenge, too. Did she really think he would take no for an answer, when he wanted her more than he had ever wanted any woman?

But Ciro knew the value of biding his time. Of waiting until the moment was right to strike—wasn't that one of the reasons why he was so successful in business? He got out of the car to open the door for her and held out his hand to assist her. After a moment of hesitation, she took it and her lips parted as their flesh made contact, as if an electric current had just passed between them. And didn't it feel exactly like that to him? It was so *physical*, this reaction between them, he thought. So uniquely *chemical*. He wanted to kiss her again, to sear his mouth against hers and remind her just what she was missing, before getting in the car and driving away.

But Lily was making him react in a way which was unfamiliar. He saw the small glance she sent towards the upstairs window and a fierce wave of something which felt like protectiveness washed over him.

'Lily,' he said softly.

She narrowed her eyes at him suspiciously. The last time he'd said her name like that she had just melted into his arms—and wasn't she tempted to do it again? 'What?'

'You know I'm happy to move your belongings into your new home? You only have to say the word and I will help in any way I can. I told you that before and nothing has changed.'

She nodded, too chewed up to speak as a terrible sadness rushed over her. What, and have him witness her emotional crumbling as she said goodbye to her old life? Watch as she embraced a future which at the moment looked bleak? Never. Never in a million years. She forced a smile. 'It's very kind of you, Ciro—but I'd rather do it on my own.'

Frustratedly, he balled his hands into two tight fists. 'Your stepmother is moving to London?'

She nodded. 'That's right.'

'So you won't have anyone round here you can rely on?'

Now was not the time to tell him that she'd never been able to rely on Suzy. That it had been a long time since she'd been able to rely on anyone. Now was the time to convince him she was going to be absolutely fine on her own—even if at that precise moment she didn't really believe it. 'I'll be okay.'

She turned to walk away but he reached

out to catch hold of her wrist—its slender paleness making his own hand look so big and dark in comparison. He could feel the urgent hammer of her pulse and the desire to hold her close was almost overwhelming. But he fought it, just as he seemed to have been fighting his feelings all evening.

'Promise me one thing,' he said.

She gave a brief laugh. 'I can't possibly promise anything until I know what it is.'

He smiled, because wouldn't he have said exactly the same thing himself in the circumstances? For a small-town girl, she certainly wasn't stupid. 'You've still got my details?'

She nodded, thinking of his cream business card, which was tucked away inside her purse.

'*Bene*. Then I want you to promise me that if you get in any trouble—with the apartment or with your brother, or *anything*—that you will come to me and let me help you. Will you do that, Lily?'

Lily hesitated. At that moment he seemed to symbolise all the things in life which she didn't have—strength and power and safety. If it had been anyone else, then she might have accepted. But she knew that there was only one reason why Ciro was offering his assistance—and that was to get her into his bed.

Her fingers tightened around her clutch bag as she shook her head. 'I appreciate your offer, Ciro, but I've already told you that I can't accept—and I meant it. Thanks again for dinner, and goodnight.'

And with that, she walked away—aware that he must still be standing there watching her because there was no sound of the car door slamming. No sound other than the sudden eerie swoop of an owl as it hooted in a distant tree.

In fact, she didn't hear his car driving away down the gravel drive until she had slipped upstairs to her room, thankfully without Suzy hearing her. Until she had peeled off the blue dress and thrown it to the ground with an uncharacteristic lack of care.

Wearing just her underwear, she stood looking in the long mirror, her fingers creeping guiltily to her breast and cupping it, just as Ciro had cupped it earlier. And she closed her eyes with sweet, remembered pleasure.

It was only then that she heard the sound of his car driving away, spraying gravel in its powerful wake.

CHAPTER SIX

THE icy water hit her face with a welcome shock and Lily was just dabbing another handful over her puffy eyes, when the doorbell rang. She stilled, cold water dripping down her fingers, thinking that she might ignore it—until she realised that it was probably only Fiona. Her boss was the only person who'd called since she had moved into the tiny apartment. Nobody else had been here apart from her brother and he…he…

Sniffing back another stupid tear, she wiped her hands and went to open the door. No point in hiding away like some sort of cave-dweller and making her sense of isolation even more complete. She pulled open the door and the breath caught in her throat as she saw who was standing on her doorstep. His dark hair was ruffled and he was dressed down in a dark T-shirt and black jeans which hugged the taut length of his thighs.

'You,' she breathed, her heart racing as she remembered his kiss in that darkened car park. Remembered the way he'd cupped her straining breast and traced the rough pad of his thumb over its puckered nipple. During that brief passionate interlude, he had made her feel like a woman again and she had *wanted* him. Oh, God, yes. She had wanted him with a fierce hunger which still haunted her.

'Me,' said Ciro, his eyes narrowing with shock as he took in her appearance—her blotchy face and puffy red eyes.

'Who let you in?'

'The other waitress. Danielle, I think her name-badge said—but what does it matter? What the hell has happened?'

'Nothing.'

'Doesn't look like nothing to me,' he observed caustically. 'You've been crying, Lily.'

'So I've been crying. So what? Should I have asked your permission first?'

Ciro scowled as a primitive urge made

him want to reach out and protect her. He wanted to haul her up against his chest and tell her not to cry. That he was going to dry her tears and make everything better. 'Can I come in?' he said.

Her lips about to frame the word 'no', Lily realised it was one of those questions which didn't really require an answer because he was walking inside and she was actually pulling the door open wider to let him pass. And that was a mistake, she realised. A big mistake. She'd thought that the apartment had looked tiny when her brother had been here at the weekend, but Ciro made it look like toy-town.

'This is *it*?' he queried incredulously.

His question voiced nothing more than her own thoughts about the size of her new home, but it hit a very raw nerve. Lily had spent three busy days decorating before Jonny's visit. She had slapped on two coats of white emulsion in an effort to make it look bigger. She had hung mirrors everywhere to reflect back the light. In the limited space available, she'd positioned pot-plants and some carefully chosen family photos and had scattered cushions over the brand-new sofa-bed. But none of her efforts had changed a thing. The flat had still looked exactly what it was—a cramped place which was much too small for a gangly teenager with sneakers the size of dustbin lids.

Not that Jonny had complained. She almost wished he had. The brave look he'd adopted had seemed too heartbreakingly old for his sixteen years. It had made her want to cry—to rail against a fate which had already robbed him of so much of his childhood. And after he'd gone back to school she had found the crumpled letter which had fallen from his rucksack—and that was when her own tears really *had* come.

'This is it,' she agreed, wishing that Ciro didn't look so infuriatingly strong and dependable as he stood in the centre of the minute sitting room. Because by some kind of weird osmosis his towering strength seemed to emphasise her own terrible sense of weakness. 'What do you want?' she croaked.

What did he want? Ciro took in the belligerent set of her mouth, which wasn't quite managing to disguise the fact that it was trembling. Her question was a pretty difficult one to answer. What would she say if she'd known that he'd been waiting for her to call after that frustrating conclusion to their dinner date? That he'd found himself looking incredulously at his mobile phone for a message which had never arrived? He'd thought that she would be unable to resist coming back for a little more of his love-making. That once she'd realised she was uselessly depriving herself of pleasure she'd see sense and come round to his way of thinking. He'd thought she would be in his bed within days. But she hadn't. There had been nothing from Lily Scott but a resounding silence.

He'd waited. And waited. Until he couldn't wait any more—and had come here today thinking that he wanted to find the quickest way into her bed. But now he wasn't sure what he wanted any more because the sight of her puffy eyes was filling him with a feeling he wasn't used to. As if he wanted to ring-fence her from trouble and keep her safe from every bad thing the world could throw at her. He frowned. So what the hell was *that* about?

'Are you going to tell me why you've been crying?' he demanded.

Lily stared at the ground, swallowing down the infuriating tears which kept springing to her eyes. 'None of your business,' she muttered.

'Lily.' And when still she didn't respond, he said her name again. 'Lily. Will you please just look at me?'

Unwillingly, she lifted her head to meet his dark gaze. 'What?'

'Why have you been crying?' he repeated.

Why did he think? She could have given him a whole list of reasons. Because it was no fun living in a place which was next door to a noisy pub. Because she was still exhausted after having done the move herself—stubbornly hiring a van which had been bigger than anything she'd ever driven before. What a nightmare it had been trying to manoeuvre the cumbersome vehicle around the village green, while all the regulars had stood outside The Duchess of Cambridge, shaking with laughter. But all these irritations had been eclipsed by her discovery that Jonny was just about to have his hopes and dreams crushed by their new-found poverty.

She shook her head, terrified that the tears would return and that this time they wouldn't stop. That they would pour down her face in an unstoppable flow and she would turn into a blubbering mess in front of him. She wanted to keep her mouth clamped tightly shut and refuse to answer and yet there was something so unyielding about him. Something so strong and determined—as if he wasn't going anywhere unless she provided some sort of answer.

She gave a small shrug. 'It's just been more difficult than I thought—moving in here. It was hard saying goodbye to the Grange, and even harder knowing what furniture to bring here.' Her stepmother had taken anything of value, of course, and most of the stuff left over had been far too large and grand to ever contemplate putting in a tiny flat above a cake shop.

Lily had managed to hang onto her mother's old writing desk and the painting of a ship which had hung in her father's study and always fascinated her when she'd been a child. Other than that, she had taken very little. Her new sitting room now contained an old, overstuffed armchair, a table which was slightly too big—and the new sofa-bed which looked completely out of place. She remembered the pitiful sight of Jonny's six-foot frame barely able to be accommodated within its cheap frame and she stared defiantly at Ciro, as if he was to blame. And he *was* to blame, she told herself fiercely. If he hadn't bought the Grange then none of this would have ever happened.

'And my brother was here this weekend,' she continued.

'Jonny?'

She was surprised he'd remembered his name and, somehow, that small touch of thoughtfulness made it even worse. She could feel that scary helplessness welling up inside her again and the tears she'd been trying to suppress started to slide remorselessly down her cheeks again.

Ciro stared at her, his face tensing. 'Lily?'

'No!' she protested, wiping a clenched fist across her face. 'It…it's not such a big deal. We'll work it out.'

'Work *what* out?'

'It d-doesn't matter.'

'Oh, believe me—it does,' he said grimly, putting his hands on her shoulders and guiding her towards the sofa and gently pushing her down onto it, before heading out of the room towards the kitchen.

'What do you think you're doing?' she called after him.

'I am making you tea. Isn't that what you English always do in times of trouble?'

The remark—delivered in his deep, Neapolitan accent—might have made her smile if the circumstances had been different. As it was, she'd never felt less like smiling and she was just blowing her nose into a sodden tissue when Ciro came back into the room, carrying a loaded tray.

He put the tray down on the table and stared at her with a stern expression. 'So what's happened with your brother which has made you cry?'

Slumped with exhaustion against the sofa, Lily watched as he poured her a cup of horribly weak tea and a terrible urge to tell him washed over her again. Maybe it was because she had bottled things up for so long that it felt as if she was threatening to explode. Or maybe it was because he just looked so determined that she suspected he wouldn't leave until she'd given him the information he wanted.

'He's been offered a place at art school.'

'Well, that's good, isn't it?' His dark eyes narrowed as she blew her nose again. 'Not the most reliable job in the world in terms of future employment, but if he's talented...'

'Yes, he's talented!' Frustratedly, she shook her head. 'And no, it isn't good.'

'Why not?'

She stared at him. Was he really so dense that he couldn't see—so that she'd be forced to spell it out for him, syllable by humiliating syllable? Maybe it was vulgar to mention the precarious state of her finances—especially to a man who had clearly never known such a predicament himself. But she knew it was too late for restraint, that she'd gone too far to stop and she needed to tell *someone*. 'Because it costs money to go and study in London. Money we haven't got.'

'You haven't got any tucked away somewhere? No stocks? Shares? That kind of thing?'

'Do you think I wouldn't already have redeemed them if I had any? When I said that my stepmother had inherited everything, I meant it.'

There was a moment of silence during which Ciro despaired at his lack of insight. Why the hell hadn't her words sunk in properly? Maybe he'd been too distracted by the sight of her heaving breasts, or the tantalising strand of hair which had flopped down around her tear-stained cheek. Or maybe he just never bothered to look at the detail of other people's lives. He knew that if she hadn't sold the Grange to him, then her stepmother would have found another buyer. But he could also see that in her emotional state, Lily might see *him* as partially responsible for her brother's thwarted dreams.

So what was he going to do about it? Given the vast resources at his disposal, couldn't he reach out to help her, even though so far she had stubbornly resisted any attempt to do so? She'd even refused his offer to provide a removal lorry and he'd heard through the grapevine that she had driven a large van rather dangerously around the village green.

She was certainly stubborn—and proud. It seemed she would rather struggle on independently than accept the assistance which he could provide. He found himself comparing her to the women he'd known in the past. He thought about Eugenia in particular—and her never-ending hunger for all things material. Yet as he looked into a pair of shimmering, bloodshot eyes he realised that Lily Scott couldn't have been more different.

Her flowery dress revealed her bare knees and her shoulders were slumped dejectedly—and in that moment she looked so damned young and *vulnerable* that he felt an aching sense of destiny deep inside him. Walking over to the sofa, he sat down beside her, seeing the startled question in her blue eyes. Slipping his arm around her, he brought her up close. 'Come here,' he said.

'Don't,' she whispered, but it was a word which lacked conviction because the truth was that it felt wonderful to be close to him again—to feel the heat of his powerful body next to hers. Only this time it wasn't sex which had brought her here—but something nearly as potent. It was safety. And solace. It was the feeling that nothing could harm her as long as Ciro was near. She felt *protected* by him—as if he could throw a charmed and protective circle around her—and that was a dangerously heady feeling. She wanted to burrow her head up against his chest, like a little animal who had found itself a safe haven. But somehow she resisted and stayed right where she was.

'Why didn't you come to me for help, Lily?' he demanded. 'When I told you that you only had to call me.'

She shook her head. 'You know why.'

He pulled her against him, so that her face was close to his neck and he realised that he was holding his breath—unsure whether she'd shy away. He felt the delicious warmth of her breath against his skin as a bitter truth washed over him. Yes, he knew why she hadn't asked him for help. Because she thought he would ask for something in return. For *sex*. Briefly, he closed his eyes. Was that true? Had he made his benevolent offer out of the goodness of his heart, or because he wanted something much more fundamental from her?

Suddenly, he was angry with himself. After years of meeting women who just wanted to get into his trousers or his bank account, he had finally met one who didn't. Who worked hard for a minimum wage and put the needs of her younger brother above her own. She hadn't fallen into bed with him, even though her hunger had easily matched his. She hadn't phoned him, or stalked him. She hadn't engineered an 'accidental' meeting in order to save face.

She had behaved like a lady from the start, while he had responded by coming onto her with the finesse of a randy soldier who hadn't been near a woman for months. He could feel the whisper of her breath on his skin, soft and rhythmical, like a warm balm. He remembered that first moment of seeing her, all warm and flushed from her baking—when the thunderbolt had hit him. He found he could imagine a child at her breast. His child. He could imagine Lily making an exemplary mother. She represented an innocent yet seductive world he had never known and suddenly he saw that it could be his. *She* could be his.

For a moment he stilled as a powerful wave of certainty washed over him and he tilted her chin upwards so that her bright eyes were looking straight at him. 'I think I'm going to have to marry you,' he said.

Blinking away the last of her tears, Lily looked at him in disbelief. For a moment she thought she must have misheard him, but the expression on his face was deadly serious. 'Have you taken leave of your senses?' she breathed.

'Maybe I have.' He shrugged. 'I don't seem to have been thinking very straight lately—but maybe that's the way it's supposed to feel when you meet a woman who is like no other woman you've known.'

'What are you talking about, Ciro?'

'I'm talking about a solution to your problems. I think you're going to have to marry me, Lily,' he said, the tip of his finger tracing a path over her suddenly trembling lips. 'Let me take care of you—and your brother. There's no need for him to turn down his place at art school—as my brother-in-law, he won't have to worry about a thing.'

Lily tried to tell herself this couldn't be real. She tried to fight against it, more as a defence mechanism than anything. But his words were unbearably tempting—and not just because she recognised that he could change Jonny's future by taking away all the doubts and uncertainty. It went deeper than that. Her thoughts were now taking her to a place which was dangerous as she acknowledged the impact this man could have on her emotions as well as her finances.

'Tell me you don't mean it,' she said, trying to inject a note of humour into her voice. 'Either you've had a knock on the head—or you've been drinking.'

He gave a low laugh. 'Neither. I *do* mean it and do you know why? Because you thrill me, Lily. You thrill me in a way I've never been thrilled by a woman before. I admire your prudence and your pride. And in a crazy kind of way, I like the fact that you refused to go to bed with me the other night.'

'Is that something which is unheard of, then?'

'Yes,' he answered simply. 'No woman has ever turned down the opportunity to have sex with me. Only you. And your old-fashioned values appeal to something fundamental in me—something which I've discovered is important. You see, I've never come across such qualities in a woman before and I may never do so again. And that's why I want you to marry me, Lily. Be my wife—and I will give you everything you need.'

Distractedly, she shook her head. 'You don't know what I need.'

'Ah, but I do, *dolcezza*. You need a man who will take care of you. Who will provide for you and let your brother fulfil his potential. While you…' He framed her face with his hands, seeing the wariness which had darkened her blue eyes. 'You can give me exactly what I want.'

She met the heated gleam of his gaze as a shiver of awareness whispered over her skin. 'And what might that be?'

He shrugged, as if he was silently acknowledging that his ideas were outmoded—

that few men would have admitted to what he was about to say. 'I want a conventional wife in a conventional role. Someone who will create a home for me. Who is waiting for me at the end of the day—not a woman fighting her way into some damned job every morning, who's too tired for dinner when she gets home. I want someone who respects her body enough to cherish it, in the way that you do. I want *you*, Lily,' he said simply. 'I've wanted you since I saw you standing in the kitchen, making pastry. I remember walking towards you and thinking that any moment I would wake up and find that I'd been dreaming. But each step which took me towards you made me realise that I was wide awake. I saw some flour on your nose and wanted to reach out and brush it away. And then you looked into my eyes and I felt the thunderbolt. I'd heard other men speak of it before, but up until that moment I didn't believe it existed. At least, not for me.'

'What thunderbolt?' she echoed in confusion, because her own memory of the day was that it had been bathed in glorious sunlight.

'In Italy we say *un colpo di fulmine.*
Literally, a bolt of lightning. It is what happens when you look at a woman and suddenly you are struck here. Here.' And he
laid his hand over his chest. 'In the heart.'

Lily could feel the deep pounding beneath her palm, aware of the significance
of what he was telling her—wanting to believe him and yet too scared to dare. Yet
hadn't she felt it, too—a powerful con-
nection when she'd seen the dark stranger
in the garden and her heart had clenched
tightly? Hadn't he seemed to symbolise
everything she'd ever wanted in a man?
He still did. But the main reason she had
pushed him away was because she was
frightened of the way he could make her
feel.

She knew only too well that feelings
made you vulnerable. They left you open to
heartbreak, and pain. She remembered how
devastated she'd been by her fiancé's sudden exit from her life and had vowed never
to put herself in that position again. And
Ciro's proposal was nothing but a whim,
she told herself fiercely. How could he possibly be offering her marriage when they

barely knew one another? It was about control and desire. About getting her into his bed, no matter what the price.

Reluctantly, she wriggled away from the warmth of his embrace and met the speculative look which gleamed from between his narrowed eyes.

'It's an amazing offer,' she said slowly. 'But it's also a crazy one—and I can't do it. I can't marry you, Ciro—and when you've had a chance to think about it, you'll thank me for it.'

CHAPTER SEVEN

BUT Ciro didn't thank Lily for turning down his proposal. On the contrary, her refusal to marry him fed a desire for her which was fast approaching fever-pitch, until he could think of nothing else. For the first time in his adult life, he had come up against something which eluded him. A woman who was strong enough to resist him. And it was driving him crazy.

He thought of Eugenia. Beautiful, high-born Eugenia, whom everyone had thought he would marry. He'd thought so himself, until he'd come to realise that her love of money and power eclipsed all the values he held so dear. He remembered the defining moment which had signalled the end, when a woman had been flirting outrageously with him at a dinner party. Eugenia had noticed, of course, but instead of showing indignation she'd hinted that she could be very 'grown up' about relationships, if he was prepared to be understanding. The implication being that he could always buy his way out of a difficult situation. That if he were ever to stray—then she would be prepared to turn a blind eye. She'd delivered the killer blow with a speculative smile. Just as long as he rewarded her with some expensive little bauble or trinket.

Eugenia's vision of the future had resembled the sophisticated bed-hopping he had witnessed as a child and it had sickened him. Ciro had ended the relationship that same night and his desire for a decent and innocent woman had been born. The cynic in him had never believed he'd find her—but now he had. Lily Scott embodied everything he'd ever dreamed of in a woman. And she had turned him down!

He began to set about changing her mind. To work out what it would take to sway her. For a man who had never had to really try—Ciro now found himself having to make an exception. But then, rising to a challenge had always been an integral part of his make-up.

He sent her flowers—a tumbling mass of blooms which were scented and white. The bouquet was accompanied by a simple, hand-written note, which read: *If I promise to behave myself, then will you have dinner with me?*

She told him afterwards that the note had made her smile—but she said it in a way which suggested that her week had been light on humour. Over dinner that night he discovered that her brother had gone back to boarding school and was about to turn down his offer of a place at art school. He saw the way her face was working, as if she was struggling to contain her emotions, and he felt an overwhelming sense of frustration, knowing that he could solve her brother's dilemma in a heartbeat. But he also knew he couldn't help her unless she was prepared to accept his help.

She told him more about her life at the Grange and he realised how difficult it must have been, living with the avaricious stepmother who had become the mistress of the house. She opened up enough to tell him that Suzy had taken stuff which had belonged to her father, which by right should have gone to Jonny. He heard her voice stumble and that was when he discovered the story of her mother's missing pearls. A beautiful and priceless necklace which had been in her family for generations.

'Let me get this straight, Lily,' he said slowly, staring into her bright blue eyes. 'You're telling me that your stepmother stole your pearls?'

Quickly, she shook her head. 'Oh, I'm sure she didn't think of it as theft. She just took them up to London and—'

'Are you expecting to ever see them again?'

She bit her lip. 'Well, no,' she admitted.

'Then that's theft,' said Ciro as a cold kind of rage filled him.

He spent the next two days in London and when he returned, he phoned Lily and asked if she'd like to go to a concert in the grounds of a nearby abbey. Her voice lifted as she accepted—almost as if she had missed him as much as he had her.

Ciro felt an immense glow of satisfaction as he got ready for the evening ahead and even the English weather seemed to be on his side. It was one of those magical summer nights, with a huge moon, and they could hear heartbreakingly beautiful strains of violin music drifting through the warm air as they walked towards the venue.

He fed her chocolate and sips of champagne and, during the interval, pulled a slim leather box from the depths of the picnic basket, where it had been nestling in a napkin.

'What's this?' she questioned as he handed it to her.

'If I were to tell you, then it would only spoil the surprise. Go on—open it.'

Lily fiddled with the clasp, the odd note in his voice making her feel suddenly nervous. She flipped up the lid, dazedly sitting back on her heels as she stared at the contents in disbelief. For there, reposing against folds of satin with a fat and creamy gleam, lay the familiar strand of pearls which had belonged to her darling mother. For a moment, her hands were shaking so much that she let the box slip from her hands and it was Ciro who retrieved it. Ciro who carefully removed the pearls and then looped them around her neck, his warm fingers brushing briefly against her skin.

'Oh, Ciro,' she whispered. Her hand reached up to touch them and for a moment she remembered her mother wearing them, looking so beautiful and elegant in those long-ago days before the cruel illness had ravaged her. Her eyes were brimming with tears as she met his compassionate look and it took a moment before she had composed herself enough to speak. 'Where did you get them?'

'Where do you think?'

'From Suzy?' And when he nodded, she blinked at him in surprise. 'She gave them to you?'

He resisted the temptation to tell her that he'd paid well over the odds for the necklace. That Suzy Scott had recognised how much he wanted them and an envious look had hardened her eyes as she'd realised why. She had asked for a sum which had been astronomical by anyone's standards but he had paid it instantly, because the thought of bartering with such a woman had filled him with distaste.

'Yes, she gave them to me.' His eyes narrowed. 'And I'm giving them back to their rightful owner.'

'Oh, *Ciro*.' She tried to find words to thank him but nothing would come—only a convulsive kind of swallowing as she realised the significance of what he'd done. What a wonderful and thoughtful gesture to have made.

'And I know it's shameless of me to strike at a moment of such high emotion, but I can be completely shameless at times.' He picked up her hand and began to brush her fingertips against his lips. 'Which is why I'm asking you again to marry me.'

'Ciro—'

'I could give you a hundred reasons why it makes sense—starting with the fact that I want to help your brother achieve his dreams by funding his place at art school.'

'That's another pretty shameless statement,' she said, shivering as she felt his tongue slide slowly against her middle finger.

He met the darkening of her eyes. 'But there are plenty of others. Top of the list is probably my insane desire to kiss you.'

She swallowed, gathering up the courage to tell him the truth. 'I think that might be near the top of my list, too.'

He moved her fingers away from his mouth and bent forward, his lips grazing hers and feeling her body shiver with desire as he pulled her close. Lacing his fingers in the thick chignon of her hair, he kissed her as he couldn't ever remember kissing a woman before—hard and deep and passionate. He heard the throaty moan she made as she wrapped her arms around his neck and felt the wild thunder of his heart. He stopped only when his lungs were so deprived of air that he felt almost lightheaded and then he drew his head away and looked down at the hectic glitter of her eyes.

'But first I need you to marry me,' he said unevenly.

And Lily knew she was all out of excuses. That it would be madness to say no—even if she wanted to. She could feel the smoothness of the pearls against her skin and she could feel her heart lifting with gratitude for what he'd done. A man like Ciro would be easy to love, she thought. Oh, so easy.

'And I need you to marry me,' she said, her voice trembling with emotion.

CHAPTER EIGHT

'I'M SCARED,' said Lily.

Staring at her ghostly image, she looked up to meet Danielle's eyes, which were reflected back at her in the silvered opal mirror. 'I know it's stupid, but I am.'

'Because?' asked Danielle patiently.

Lily touched her fingers to the exquisite veil which flowed down over her shoulders and the woman in the mirror mimicked the movement. Would it sound crazy to admit to feeling lost in Il Baia—this vast Neapolitan hotel of Ciro's, where she and Danielle had been staying in the days leading up to today's ceremony? Or to try to explain that the beautiful city of Naples and strange language were a complete culture shock to someone who'd spent most of her life in and around Chadwick Green? It was as if the reality of Ciro's wealthy life and powerful influence had only just sunk in and she wondered whether she would be equipped to deal with it. In the passion of the moment, it had been all too easy to say yes to his proposal of marriage—but here in the sumptuous confines of his life, she wondered how she would cope with being his wife.

She shrugged and the delicate silk of the bodice whispered over her shoulders. 'I can't imagine living here in Naples.'

Danielle made a minor adjustment to the wreath of white roses which sat on top of Lily's piled up hair. 'Oh, Lily,' she said, her voice as briskly cheerful as it had been all morning. 'All that will change with time. You've got to give yourself a chance. It's just normal pre-marital nerves, that's all.'

Was it? Lily wondered. Her mother's pearls gleamed softly at her neck and her heart was beating out a strange new rhythm as she gazed at herself in all her wedding finery. Did all brides feel this way? As if they were poised on a very high diving board but not quite sure how deep the water beneath them was? Probably not. But then, most brides knew their husband far more intimately than she knew Ciro.

She had thought that once she'd agreed to marry him he would want to consummate their relationship, but that hadn't been the case. He wanted to hold off until their wedding night. He told her he loved the fact that she'd refused him. That it made her different from every woman he'd ever known. He told her that he found it a *challenge* to wait—that his desire for her was building and building with every day that passed.

The waiting game was almost over and tonight was the big night—when they would be joined together in the most fundamental way of all. But Lily wished this terrible sense of foreboding would leave her. The sense that something was slightly off kilter. Was it because she still hadn't plucked up the courage to tell him about her relationship with Tom—even though Tom no longer mattered? She'd kept putting it off and putting it off, unwilling to cast any shadows over the sunny days leading up to the wedding. And now she'd left it so long, it was too late. The bride wasn't even supposed to *see* her husband until she met him at the altar—so what was she supposed to do? Text him now and tell him she'd once been engaged to another man?

'I don't know if I can go through with it, Dani,' she said hoarsely.

'Of course you can.' Danielle brushed down the skirt of her blush-pink bridesmaid dress and smiled. 'Because in a church not far from here awaits the kind of man most women would kill to marry. Think about it this way. You're in a beautiful city, staying in an amazing five-star hotel overlooking the bay—a hotel which happens to be owned by the man who will soon be your husband. You're in *Naples*, for God's sake—and about to marry one of its most famous residents! It's normal for a bride to feel scared before she walks down the aisle—but you have more reason than most to do so.'

'I do?'

'Of course you do! You're a foreigner here—and it's going to take a while before you feel like you fit in. Just don't expect too much.'

Once more, Lily touched the pearls at her neck. 'I don't think his mother likes me.'

'Why not?'

Lily recalled Leonora D'Angelo's demeanour when Ciro had taken her round to be introduced. The way she had presented two cool cheeks to be kissed, before looking her up and down with narrow-eyed assessment. And Lily had felt like a galumphing giant in comparison to the perfectly groomed and elegant woman who sat dwarfed in an enormous chair.

Everything in the dimly lit Neapolitan apartment had seemed so *fragile* and it had made her move carefully, almost exaggeratedly—as if afraid that a sudden move might knock over one of the priceless-looking antiques which adorned the room. And hadn't there been a noticeable lack of affection between mother and son? Ciro's cool attitude towards his mother seemed to have been more *dutiful* than loving. For a moment that had scared the hell out of Lily and she wasn't sure why.

'She seemed to disapprove of me,' she said.

'Well, that's a relief!' Danielle grinned.

'No mother on the planet ever approves of her son's bride—that's a given! They're always as jealous as hell until the requisite replacement boy-child makes an appearance. What did she say?'

Lily stared down at her glittering sapphire and diamond engagement ring. She couldn't blame the awkward atmosphere on the language barrier since Ciro's mother spoke English as perfectly as her son. She had just felt *wrong*. As if her pale, English curves would never fit into the sleek and moneyed world which the D'Angelos inhabited.

But if she was being honest, it was more than Leonora D'Angelo's attitude which had given her cause for concern. His cousin Giuseppe, who was to be their best man, seemed to have reservations about her, too. Ciro had told her that the two men were very close—more like brothers than cousins. But over dinner, the handsome blue-eyed Giuseppe had seemed to be studying her intently—as if he was trying to work her out. Or had her pre-wedding nerves just imagined that?

'So are you saying you want me to go

and talk to Ciro?' Danielle's voice broke
into her worried thoughts and Lily watched
as her friend walked over to the window
and stared out at the blue sweep of the bay.
'In front of the two hundred assembled
guests who will be filing into the church,
even as we speak—and somehow explain
to him that you've changed your mind
about marrying him?'

For a few seconds, Lily allowed herself
to play out the scene in her head—imagining the uproar and embarrassment as all
the guests turned to one another in horrified question. And that was when she
started laughing at the ridiculousness of
it all. What was she *like*? Wasn't this what
she'd secretly been dreaming about, almost from the first time she'd seen him?
When her heart had tumbled into a place
she hadn't been expecting—and she had
connected with him in a way which had
taken her completely by surprise? Wasn't
this the end-product of weeks of frustration and years of yearning—that soon she
would have someone to love? Someone who
seemed to need all the love she could give
him—because she thought she detected a

great core of loneliness at the very heart of Ciro D'Angelo. The man who seemed to have everything except for the one thing that money couldn't buy.

'No, I haven't changed my mind, Dani. And you're right. It's just stupid nerves which made me forget just how lucky I am.' She stood up and the layers of white tulle fell to the ground in a soft whisper. 'Come on, let's go—because I'm not sure whether it's the done thing in Italy for the bride to be late and I have a very nervous brother next door, who has been railroaded into giving me away!'

Lily was much too nervous and excited to take much notice of the bustling streets during the short drive to the church and she listened to Jonny and Danielle's excited comments with only half an ear. But as the car drew up outside the small church she felt a strange sense of approaching destiny.

There was a sudden hush as she stood in the arched doorway of the small church, dimly aware of the overpowering scent of flowers and the sudden swell of organ music. For a moment she was aware of the enormity of the step she was about to take, before reassuring herself that was perfectly normal, too. Because it *was* important. One of the most important days of her life.

Smoothing down her veil, she looped her arm through Jonny's and began the slow walk down the aisle, aware of the collective turning of heads as she passed the people who were mostly strangers to her. But there was only one person in her line of vision. One person who dominated it all. Who had dominated her life from the minute he'd walked into it on a sunny English day.

Toweringly dark and impossibly gorgeous—there seemed almost an *edge* to him today. It was as if the impeccably formal clothes had distanced him and made him into someone different—someone she didn't really know. He was at home here, Lily thought suddenly. At home among all these sleek and sophisticated people, while she was the pale Englishwoman who knew nobody. Her heart missed a beat and for a moment she felt as if she couldn't go through with it, her step faltering slightly as her white shoe stepped into a pool of rainbow light which poured down from the stained glass window. She saw Jonny glance at her, his gaze concerned.

And then the man waiting at the altar slowly turned his head and Lily's heart fired into life again, crashing against her ribcage so hard that she wondered if the movement was visible beneath her delicate dress.

This is Ciro, she thought—and felt a soft, creeping pleasure as she walked towards him, looking up to meet the dark blaze of his eyes as she finally reached him. The man she had grown to admire and to respect. Who had somehow got back her mother's pearls and sternly told her that it would be a crime if her talented brother didn't achieve his potential. The man who had done so many loving things to get her here today. Her darling Ciro.

'Okay?' he mouthed at her, and she nodded, sliding her hand into the waiting warmth of his.

The service was conducted in both languages and Lily managed to repeat her vows without stumbling—though her finger was trembling as Ciro slid the golden

ring onto it. And then the priest was pro-
nouncing them man and wife and the con-
gregation had started clapping and he put
his face close to hers, a smile nudging at
the edges of his lips.

'You look beautiful,' he murmured.

'Do I?'

'More than beautiful. Like a flower. Soft
and pure and white—like the Lily you were
named after.'

'Oh, Ciro,' she whispered.

He smiled. Her face was upturned, her
lips trembling with eagerness, but the kiss
he grazed over her lips was breathtakingly
short and deliberately so. They still had
a wedding breakfast and reception to get
through before they could be alone as man
and wife. And he had waited much too long
for this to want to do anything but savour
her at his leisure. 'Come on, let us go and
meet our guests,' he said.

The reception and the first night of their
honeymoon were being held at the Il Baia
hotel which had the added pressure of everyone falling over themselves to please
Ciro. Lily had wondered if he wouldn't
rather spend his wedding night anony-

mously, rather than in a place where everyone knew him—but he had shaken his head.

'It means we can slip away from the reception without making a fuss,' he'd murmured. 'And it wouldn't be a very good advertisement for the hotel if the boss spent his wedding night in a rival establishment, now would it?'

Lily supposed it wouldn't, and by early evening, she couldn't have cared less where they were going—she just couldn't wait to get there. Her face ached from all the photo-taking, she'd shaken a million hands during the line-up and she'd barely managed to get close to a morsel of food, let alone eat any of it. She tried not to be overwhelmed by the vast amount of Ciro's friends, compared to the small clutch of people she'd flown out from Chadwick Green. And she tried not to feel insecure when she looked at all the beautiful women who chattered so vivaciously, expressively swirling their hands around as they talked.

At least Jonny seemed to be enjoying himself with a group of Ciro's younger cousins, while Danielle was certainly get-

ting plenty of offers to dance. And Fiona Weston was eating some sort of dessert called *sfogliatella*, and trying very hard to find the recipe for it.

By nine o'clock, when Lily was in serious danger of flagging, Ciro put his arm around her waist.

'I think it's about time I took you to my bed at last,' he murmured. 'How does that idea appeal to you, Signora D'Angelo?'

She leaned her head against his broad shoulder, thrilling to the possessive note in his voice and to the sound of her brand-new title. She was Ciro's *wife*, she thought ecstatically and all her uncertainties melted away. For the first time in a long time she would have someone to lean on. Someone who would be watching out for her as she would be watching out for him. Someone whom she could love and support in turn. Her *partner*, in every sense of the term. 'Oh, yes, please,' she whispered.

'Then let's slip away—without any fuss.'

A glass elevator zoomed them up to the honeymoon suite, which was situated at the very top of the beautiful building. As they stepped inside Lily became aware of a large

salon with elegant sofas, lavish displays of flowers and a bucket containing champagne which had been placed there for the newlyweds. Terracotta tiles led outside to a flower-filled terrace and beyond that was a breathtaking view of the bay, under the ever-watchful eye of Mount Vesuvius.

'It's exactly like looking at a picture from a travel brochure,' she exclaimed as she stared at the dramatic outline of the famous volcanic mountain.

But the views and the luxury were forgotten the moment her husband took her into his arms, his lips brushing lightly against hers, and Lily could feel his incredible restraint as he pulled her close to his aroused body.

'I feel I've waited for ever for this night,' he said unsteadily.

'Me, too.' She put her arms around his neck. 'And now it's here.'

'And now it's here,' he repeated. 'Are you nervous?'

She thought about his experience. About what he might expect of her. And once again she felt a brief pang of unease as she wondered whether she should have told

him. But how *could* she come out and say it, especially now? 'A little,' she answered truthfully.

'Some nerves are perfectly natural, but I will show you that there is nothing to be scared of.' His smile was reassuring as he gestured towards the ice-bucket. 'Would you like a glass of champagne?'

Aware of an increasing feeling of trepidation, Lily shook her head, carefully removing the wreath of roses and the veil which was still pinned tightly to her head. She hung the veil over the back of a chair and looked at him. Was it madness to find herself thinking that she just wanted to get this bit over with? As if this was a necessary hurdle to clear—so that afterwards they could relax properly and just enjoy the rest of the honeymoon and their life together?

'Can we just go to bed, Ciro?' she blurted out. 'Please.'

His momentary surprise was eclipsed by an intense feeling of satisfaction. Shyness and eagerness—could there be a more perfect combination? 'Oh, Lily,' he murmured. 'My beautiful, innocent bride—for whom

I have waited as I have waited for no other woman.' Ignoring her small squeal of protest, he picked her up and carried her into the bedroom, his arms sinking into the massed layers of her tulle skirt before setting her down on the cool, marble floor.

'I want you to do something for me,' he said as he slid the zip of her dress down in one fluid movement and it sank to the ground like a fresh fall of snow.

'Anything,' she whispered. She stepped out from the circle of the discarded gown so that she stood before him in just her white lacy bra, her thong panties, a pair of lace-topped stockings and matching suspender belt. The high white silk wedding shoes made her much taller than usual and they made her stand differently, too, so that the jut of her hips seemed to be on display, and she saw his eyes darken.

'Let down your hair,' he said suddenly.

'My hair?'

'You realise that I've never seen your hair loose before?' he questioned unevenly. 'And somehow it seems symbolic that it should be tonight when you set it free.'

His dark eyes were blazing with *won-*

der...as if all this was very new for him and of course, it was. And Lily realised just what it was that made marriage so special and profound. He had never done this before and neither had she. Made love to her *spouse*—which happened to be a very old-fashioned word, but in that moment she *felt* old-fashioned. And that was how Ciro liked her to be, wasn't it?

Lifting her hand to the intricate topknot, she pulled out the first pin and dropped it onto an adjacent table as the first shiny strand tumbled down. Ciro sucked in a breath as the second pin was removed, and then a third—and as each one liberated another thick lock it was accompanied by the tinny whisper of each falling pin.

His throat was bone-dry by the time she'd finished and his groin was threatening to explode. She looked like a goddess, he thought. Like a creature who represented the fields and the harvest—with that glorious corn-coloured spill of hair.

'Promise me something?' he questioned.

Her eyes met his and she tilted him a smile. 'You know where I stand on promises, Ciro.'

'Ah, but this is one you can easily keep, *dolcezza mia*. Promise me that you'll never cut your hair.'

For a moment, she hesitated. He made it sound as if her long, cascading hair was what defined her—and something about that made her feel faintly uneasy. Yet the look of appraisal which was making his dark eyes gleam like jet quickly had her nodding her head in agreement. 'Okay, I promise,' she said softly.

'Mille grazie,' he murmured as he pulled her close, framing her face in his hands before lowering his mouth to hers.

He kissed her until she moaned. Until he felt her weaken in his arms and then he picked her up and carried her over to the bed, laying her down on its centre, before removing her shoes and dropping them to the floor. For a moment he thought of leaving her wearing her provocative underwear. If it had been anyone other than Lily, he would have done just that. But she was not one in a long line of lovers who always tried to outperform themselves in order to please him. He did not need the titillation of seeing her curvaceous body encased in scanty pieces of silk and lace—he wanted to see her naked. To feel her naked. As close as it was possible for a man and woman to be. Because this was his wife. His *wife*.

Wriggling his hand behind her back, he unclipped her bra, a shuddered sigh escaping from his lips as her lush breasts were freed of their lacy confinement. Dipping his head, he started to suckle her and a shaft of pleasure shot through him as he circled his tongue around each pert nipple. Hooking his fingers into her panties, he slid them down over her thighs—unable to resist the brief brush of his thumb against her clitoris, smiling at the squeal of pleasure she gave in response.

'Ciro,' she breathed, her fingers scrabbling wildly at his shoulders.

Her fervour pleased him almost as much as her body, but he realised that, although she was now naked, he was still fully dressed and so he backed away from the bed.

'Don't move,' he instructed as he saw her mouth begin to form a circle of objection. 'I need to get rid of these damned clothes.'

'I'm not going anywhere,' she whispered.

'Good,' he said, unbuttoning his shirt with fingers which were shaking like a drunk's.

Lily's heart pounded as she watched him undress, carelessly tossing his jacket onto a nearby chair in a way she suspected was uncharacteristic. Because even in jeans, he somehow always managed to look immaculate. Maybe that was an Italian thing. 'Shouldn't you hang that up?' she questioned nervously as his white shirt fluttered to the ground.

Pausing midway through easing his trouser zip down over his aching hardness, Ciro registered the sudden shyness in her voice and he gave a low laugh as he pulled his trousers off and wriggled out of his boxers.

'If you think,' he said as he joined her on the bed and pulled her warm and compliant body into his arms, 'that I am capable of anything right now other than maybe this…'

This was a kiss. A kiss which seemed to go on for ever. Which made the world shift and blur, leaving Lily a helpless victim of her senses. He moved his lips away and began to touch her breasts, his fingers drifting in provocative circles over her aroused flesh. She felt his hand skate proprietorially over the flat of her stomach and her eyes flew open to find that he was watching her, his dark gaze fiercely intent. 'Oh, Ciro,' she breathed.

'What is it, *angelo mio*?' he murmured, moving his hand down and rubbing his fingers luxuriously against the soft bush of curls.

'Oh, Ciro, I..." His thumb flicked across the engorged button of flesh which was concealed beneath the damp tangle and she gave a moan of pleasure because this was just *bliss*. She felt all the worries of the past recede. She saw nothing ahead but a bright and gloriously golden future. And Ciro was responsible. He was the one who had taken her fortunes and turned them around. The man who had picked her up when she was at her lowest ebb. Who had seen something in her. Something good. Something he liked enough to make him want her as his wife. He had scooped her up and made her feel safe and, now that the nerves of the wedding ceremony had passed, she could concentrate on all the glorious possibilities of the present. An overwhelming sense of *gratitude* washed over her and so did something else. Something which was bubbling up inside her and which felt too big and too important to hold back. Something she could give to him, with all her heart, if she dared to open the floodgates. 'Ciro?'

'What is it, *dolcezza*?'

'I…I love you,' she whispered.

There was a pause. 'Of course you do,' he murmured. And even though countless women had said it to him in the past, even though he had always dismissed the pat little sentence as meaningless—her declaration pleased him. Because she was his wife and she *should* love him. Just as he would love her in every way he could.

Lily's lips were tracing heated little kisses across his throat and he realised that they hadn't even discussed contraception— but that, for once, it really didn't matter. She was his wife. If she got pregnant, so what? Wasn't that what marriage was all about? He moved over her, touching his mouth to hers, feeling his erection pushing against her belly—and it was bigger and harder than he could ever remember feeling before. *Dio*—but this was so close to pleasure that it almost felt like *pain*. And not just in his body—for wasn't there an unfamiliar ache deep in his heart as he looked at her?

'I don't want to wear protection,' he said, his voice shaking as he made this unusually candid admission. 'I want to feel you. Just *you*, Lily. My skin against your skin. My hardness against your softness. No barrier, *mio angelo*—no barrier at all.'

'Then don't,' she said shakily, her arms wrapping around his broad back, her lips kissing his neck—inhaling the raw, citrusy smell of him, scarcely able to believe this was happening. 'Don't wear anything. Just…make love to me, Ciro. Please. Or else I think I'm going to die with the wanting.'

For a split second, something inside him jarred. Was it the sudden urgency of her words which surprised him—or just the assertive way she had expressed them? Yet Ciro knew he should rejoice in the fact she was relaxed—because wasn't tension supposed to be the enemy of a virgin's enjoyment? He splayed one hand luxuriously over her peaking breast while the other positioned himself to where she was wet and waiting. He could feel the powerful roar of his blood as it pounded senselessly around his veins and her wide blue eyes looked straight up into his.

'Lily,' he said, and entered her, his body taut with restraint as her velvet heat enclosed him.

'Ciro,' she breathed.

He saw her eyes close, saw her body shudder as he began to move, slowly at first, but gradually thrusting deeper and deeper—deeper than he'd thought he could ever go. Never had any woman ever felt so sweet nor so delicious—but then, never had he felt this aroused. 'I'm not hurting you?' he gasped.

The sweet rhythm had been consuming her, but now Lily's eyes snapped open to see his eyes searching her face—as if wanting clues about how much pleasure he was giving her. Hurting her? Why, nothing could be further from the truth. She didn't think that anything had ever given her so much pleasure as this *intimacy* of being joined with her husband. Her beloved husband. Instinctively, she gave a great bubbling sound of laughter as her arms looped around his neck, her bent legs lifting to entwine themselves around his broad back.

'Hurting me?' she murmured as she jutted her hips against him with practised ease. 'God, no. It's…it's…oh, Ciro—it's *amazing.*'

A hint of darkness momentarily clouded his overwhelming pleasure—but the writhing thrust of Lily's hips against his swollen hardness was enough to suck him right back in there again. He groaned as he juggled pleasure with restraint. It was torture holding back like this but Ciro knew he must temper his hunger. Because didn't they say it took virgins longer to achieve orgasm? And there was no way his new wife was going to miss out on *that* on her wedding night.

But suddenly she was clinging to him, her thighs digging into his sweat-sheened back as if she were riding a horse. Suddenly, her lips were torn away from his as she tipped her head back with an exultant moan—and he watched the telltale arching of her back as she started to come.

He waited only for her shuddering orgasm to fade and then Ciro let go completely. He heard the disbelieving cry which seemed to come from somewhere deep inside him. Felt the exquisite contractions which forced all the seed pumping from his body, straight into her wet and pulsing warmth.

Perhaps he might still not have guessed—at least, not then. He was so silken-deep in pleasure that he might simply have closed his eyes and drifted off to sleep, had Lily not begun to wriggle her toes up and down the sides of his body with an erogenous agility which spoke volumes. The rapturous aftermath of his orgasm began to disintegrate, like the lick of the incoming tide against a sandcastle built on the edge of the sea. He spanned his hands over her hips and lifted her slightly away from him so that their eyes were on a collision course, but Ciro was careful not to accuse. Because he might simply be mistaken. Please God, may he be mistaken.

'You liked that?' he questioned softly.

'You know I did,' she whispered, wishing that he'd bring her back down on top of him so that she could carry on kissing him.

There was a heartbeat of a pause. 'You know, for a minute back then I almost thought that you were…experienced.'

The word was used almost casually, but Lily wasn't a fool. She could hear the faint brittleness which underpinned it, even if she hadn't been able to see the sudden hard glitter of his eyes. She bit her lip, searching for the right words to say, but she couldn't seem to find them anywhere.

'*Are* you, Lily?' he questioned softly. 'Are you experienced?'

There was a pause. 'Not very,' she admitted.

'Not *very*?' He stared at her, disbelief welling up inside him like a bitter tide. For a moment he thought that he might be mistaken. That it was something which was lost in translation between two people who spoke different languages. But the shrinking look in her eyes told a different story. Naked, without the prim clothes which made you think of wholesomeness and innocence— Ciro realised he was seeing the real Lily for the very first time. The flesh which he'd only ever seen covered with retro clothes was as creamy and as delicious as he'd imagined. The hair which he'd found so alluring now spilled gloriously over the pillow, just like every fantasy he'd ever had. But now it seemed to mock him because the image she'd presented was nothing but an illusion and he felt the kick of pain in his heart as he registered just how *wanton* she looked.

Yet why should he be so surprised? Why had he ever thought she was different from all the others, when it turned out that she was exactly the same? He remembered his own mother—too wrapped up in her own desires to spare much time for the little boy who waited alone in the big, cold mansion. Remembered his nameless fears as he'd lain awake night after night and wondered if she would return home alone or not. He remembered Eugenia and the way she'd hinted that sexual straying was *negotiable*. Had he thought he'd found illusive innocence in the wholesome-looking Lily—only to discover that he had been duped all along?

He felt the violent slam of his heart against his ribcage but he asked the question anyway. Knowing that he was nothing but a crazy fool to cling onto a last shred of hope as he looked deep into her blue eyes. 'So were you a virgin, Lily?' he bit out painfully. 'Or was your bridal innocence nothing but a sham?'

CHAPTER NINE

LILY'S heart sank as she met the dark accusation which blazed from Ciro's eyes.
His hands were digging into her hips; she
wondered if he realised that—or whether
her skin was just more sensitive than usual
because of the amazing orgasm he'd just
given her. It shouldn't *matter* whether
or not she was a virgin, she told herself
fiercely, and yet hot on the heels of that
thought came another. *Stupid* Lily for not
having told him sooner. Stupid, stupid, *stupid*. And how best to tell him now, in these
awful circumstances? When they were
both stark naked and he was staring at her
with an expression she'd never seen on his
face before and would be quite happy never
to see again.

'No, I wasn't a virgin. But then…' she

tried a smile which didn't quite come off '…neither were you.'

A fierce pain shafted through his heart and his throat felt as if it had been dusted with gravel. 'Ah, but I never pretended to be otherwise, did I? Unlike you.'

He pushed her away from him, positioning her against the rumpled bank of pillows before getting up off the bed—as if he wanted to put as much distance between them as possible.

'I didn't *pretend*!' she protested, the cool air rushing over her bare skin and making her acutely aware of his physical absence.

'Didn't you?' He flicked her a contemptuous look as he reached for his boxer shorts. 'You certainly didn't bother to correct my assumption that you were innocent, did you, Lily? Nor bother enlightening me that you'd had other lovers before me— other men who have been *intimate* with your body. You went along with it, didn't you?'

Lily bit her lip as his words hit a nerve, knowing that he was speaking the truth. She *had* let herself go along with it for all kinds of reasons. She'd known that he respected her *because* she'd kept him at a distance. That women who didn't fall into bed with him were something of a rarity in his life. And she hadn't seemed able to stop herself from buying into his fantasy. She'd liked the way he made her feel. She'd liked it too much. He had made her feel cherished—as if there *had* been no man before him. He still did. Tom was like a shadow in comparison. Couldn't she make him understand that?

'I know I should have told you,' she said carefully. 'I know that now. But it was so easy to go along with the amazing time we were having and I didn't want to spoil what we had.'

'So you thought you'd wait until our wedding night to spring your little surprise on me, did you? Until you'd ridden me like a hooker? Forgive me if I don't commend your sense of timing.' He saw her flinch at his crude statement, but he didn't care because the dull, blunting pain of betrayal was hurting his heart. 'How many was it, Lily?' He held up his hand, where his golden wedding ring seemed to catch the light and mock him. 'Less than the fingers on one hand—or is that a conservative estimate? As many as fifty, maybe? No wonder you were so damned good!'

'Not lovers in the *plural*!' she cried, cringing beneath the contempt in his dark eyes as he started sliding the silken boxer shorts over the taut length of his thighs. 'There's been only one before you!'

'And that's supposed to make me happy?'

Looking at him, she couldn't imagine that anything would make him happy right then. Unless some last-ditch attempt at logic might appeal to his wounded sense of pride. 'You didn't tell me about your previous lovers.'

'Not in detail, no—but I certainly didn't twist the truth to make myself into something I wasn't.'

She sucked in a deep breath, knowing that she needed to confront what lay at the bottom of all this. 'Was my supposed virginity so important to you, then, Ciro?' she questioned quietly.

There was a moment's silence as he met her bright blue gaze but he hardened his heart to it. 'You know it was,' he said coldly as a pulse began to flicker at his temple.

He watched as her fingers grabbed at the rumpled sheet, bringing it up to cover the soft blur of curls at her thighs. And he realised that she was no different from any other woman—willing to stoop to any deception if she thought she was in with a chance of hooking a wealthy man.

Eugenia had made it clear that she would overlook anything, just as long as she was adequately rewarded—but at least she had been *honest* about her motives. She hadn't pretended to be a sweet innocent, acting as if butter wouldn't melt in that delicious mouth of hers. Cleverly buying into his ultimate fantasy of marrying a woman who was a virgin.

'Ciro, come back to bed. Please.'

His mouth twisted. 'What a fool I've been,' he grated. 'A fool to have been sucked in by your soft curves and homespun talents. By your supposed innocent primness.' He picked up his discarded shirt and slid it on over his broad shoulders. 'The first and only woman who didn't allow me to seduce her. My ideal woman, or so I thought.'

Lily flinched, holding her hands out towards him in a gesture of supplication. 'I should have told you,' she said, watching as he pulled on his trousers. 'But I didn't, and you never actually asked me. And Tom wasn't—'

'Tom?' he bit out.

'He was the man I was going to marry.'

'You were actually going to *marry* him?'

'Yes,' she admitted. 'But he called the wedding off when he met someone else.'

'When?'

'Two days before it was supposed to happen.'

Some deeply buried shred of compassion implored Ciro to offer her sympathy for having been jilted. Some small inner voice called to him and asked whether her experience might have affected the way she had subsequently behaved with him. But his sense of being wronged was so great that he did not heed it. The pain in his heart was far too strong to contemplate any easy forgiveness towards her. He had been brought up to suspect the motives of women and Lily Scott had just reinforced his judgement. 'And did he thrill you?' he questioned, walking towards the bed and towering over her as he finished buckling his belt.

Lily stared up at him, her heart beating with a mixture of fear and excitement—wanting more than anything that he would just take his trousers off again and get back into bed with her and…and…

'Did he, Lily?' he demanded, his heated question breaking into her shockingly erotic thoughts. 'Did he thrill you? Did he make you come when he touched you?'

She knew that she should answer his outrageous question truthfully. That there could now be nothing but complete honesty between them, if there was to be any chance of salvaging this. Who was to say that something good couldn't rise from the ashes of this terrible showdown they'd had? But not at any cost. Because there was no way she could answer something like that with any degree of dignity. And besides, she wasn't able to give him the only answer he wanted to hear. 'I don't think you have any right to ask me something like that,' she said quietly.

He turned away, sick with disgust at himself—and sick with jealousy, too—her refusal to answer telling him everything he needed to know. Because he had wanted her to blurt out that she had never known pleasure before him. That no other man had made her cry out in helpless rapture. But they had, hadn't they? This man *Tom*. The man who had abandoned her. Who had taken the virginity which should have been *his* to take.

'I should have listened to Giuseppe,' he said bitterly.

Lily's ears pricked up at the mention of the cousin who had looked at her so assessingly, his blue eyes narrowed with suspicion. 'Why, what did he say?'

He shook his head. 'That you sounded too good to be true. But I blocked my ears to it all.' His laugh was bitter. 'And I fell for your pretty play-acting. Your outraged behaviour when I pushed you up against the car when the reality was that you were gagging for it.'

Her hand flew to her mouth. 'How dare you say that?'

'Because it's *true*!' All true, he thought grimly. His pure and prim Lily had been nothing but an illusion—a woman he'd conjured up from the depths of some bizarre fantasy. He felt the cold clamp of a nameless emotion as it closed round his heart, sealing up cracks which had started to appear when he'd met her. Slipping on his socks and shoes, he picked up his jacket from where he'd flung it over the chair, then hunted around until he had located his car keys.

The jangling of metal brought Lily to her senses. 'Where are you going?' she questioned.

'Out!'

'Ciro—'

'Before I say or do something I may later regret,' he said, turning away from her distress and from those blue eyes which were now brimming with unshed tears. Wrenching open the door, he slammed his way out of the suite.

Lily's heart was pounding so hard that she lay back weakly against the pillows, her eyes fixed on the closed door, praying for him to come back. To take her in his arms and to tell her that he was sorry he'd lost it. To tell her that he'd been unreasonable and could they please just forget it had ever happened and start over.

He didn't, of course. The minutes ticked by with excruciating slowness until an hour had passed, and then another. Through the open shutters she could hear the faint drift of music and laughter. And the irony didn't escape her that downstairs people were still celebrating their wedding, while upstairs the bride lay alone in the honeymoon bed.

She glanced at the ornate clock hanging on the far wall to see that it was well past midnight. Where *was* he? It dawned on her that he could be in any one of a hundred places she didn't know about. Because she knew so little of his life here. And in that moment, Lily realised how alone she was. Alone in a strange city, having married one of its major players—and then been abandoned by him in the most bitter of rows.

What the hell was she going to do?

For a moment her fingers twisted at the sheet, her mind spinning with possibilities until she came to a sudden decision, motivated by something which had defined her life so far. Something called survival.

Was she going to lie there feeling sorry

for herself because Ciro D'Angelo had judged her so negatively? No way. Just because she'd let all his harsh accusations wash over her, didn't mean she had to continue being a mindless *victim*. She picked up her phone and punched out his number, but wasn't surprised when it went straight through to voicemail. She left a message in a surprisingly calm voice—saying that she didn't think it was a good idea to go driving in the middle of the night when he was clearly in such a volatile mood. And could he please just let her know he was safe.

Half an hour later, a stark two-word text came winging back.

I'm safe.

And that was that. Lily was left in the vast suite without a clue where he was, or when he'd be coming back. It promised to be a long night. She had nowhere to go, she realised as she slithered into the warmth of an oversized bathrobe—and no one she could talk to. All the people closest to her were here at the hotel—but she could hardly go knocking on Danielle's door in the middle of the night to tell her that she'd been deserted by her new husband. Apart from the shame of admitting something like that, wasn't there still part of her which was hoping that once Ciro had calmed down they could talk about this like adults and maybe get round it?

Yes, she'd been wrong not to tell him about her past—but surely he could understand why she had allowed herself to be swept along by the romance and security he'd been offering her? He'd said he *wanted* to help her, and he had gone all out to get her to agree with him. Did that count for nothing—and was he now going to deny the existence of the lightning flash of attraction which had hit them both? Surely their future didn't have to be governed by something as unimportant as her virginity.

But it was important to him, she realised. It was important in a primitive way which most men wouldn't admit to. In the same way he'd admitted to all that stuff about wanting a wife who would always be waiting for him.

She must have fallen asleep because when she awoke, the suite was filled with the pale apricot light of dawn. Slowly she sat up in bed, her heart almost leaping out of her chest when she saw the dark figure who was seated at the other side of the room, silently watching her. He had removed his jacket and wore his white shirt and dark wedding trousers. But his feet were bare, his eyes were blank and his mouth was tight and unsmiling.

Suppressing a shiver, Lily ran her hand through the mussed tangle of her hair. 'Where have you been?'

'Out.'

She didn't react. So was this how it was going to be from now on? She wanted to hurl herself at him, to demand to know whether he had sought refuge in the arms of another woman. Someone who would soothe him and be indignant that he'd been short-changed by his bride. But Lily knew that misplaced emotion and unfounded fears weren't going to help her at a time like this. That if there was any hope of salvaging this whole mess, then she needed to be calm. To show him that she could still be strong. More importantly, that she cared about him. 'I was worried about you.'

'Why?'

'Because you drove off in such a rage—

for all I knew, you could have had some kind of accident.'

'And wouldn't that have made it easier for you?' he asked, in a flat, deadly voice.

'E-easier for me? What are you talking about?'

'Billionaire groom's car plummets off coastal road,' he intoned, still in that same flat tone—like a radio commentator making a sombre announcement. 'Leaving his bride of less than twenty-four hours a widow.'

'Ciro! That's a terrible thing—'

'The operative word being *billionaire*, of course,' he mused. 'The widow takes it all—the money, the houses, the share portfolio. Wouldn't that be the perfect solution, Lily? After all, you were prepared to pretend to be something you weren't in order to secure a marriage to a rich man. Maybe you've been praying to get my money sooner rather than later?'

'Stop it,' she breathed.

He shook his head with an air of disbelief, like a man who had just emerged unscratched from the wreckage of a plane. 'But I guess I have nobody to blame but myself for what's happened. For once in my life, I was completely blinkered. So blinkered that I walked straight into your honeyed trap—though if I'd stopped to think about it, it was glaringly obvious what you were trying to do. You were so desperate to secure your house and your future—'

'And you were so desperate to be the first man to lay claim to my body,' she flared back, reeling at all the emotional ammunition he was firing at her.

'Yes. Yes, I was.' He stared at her, as if trying to make sense of it. 'I am an experienced man of the world and usually I can see right through any form of deception. But I have to say that you really got me, Lily. You were so…*wondering*. So unbelievably sweet. Like it was the first time for you.'

'Because that's what it felt like!' she protested, her voice trembling now. 'It really was like that.'

He leapt on her words, like a hungry dog on a bone. 'So you didn't feel anything for the other man you were engaged to?'

She bit her lip. It would have been so easy to say no. That she'd felt nothing at all for Tom—but that would have been a lie. And there weren't going to be any more lies. No matter how awful the consequences, she could no longer shy away from the truth. 'Yes, of course I did,' she whispered.

Ciro stood up as if he'd been struck—the pain nearly as bad as it had been last night when he'd discovered that another man had been the first to give her pleasure. He walked over to the double doors which were open to the spacious terrace, beyond which the dawn-washed bay glittered beneath the rising sun. This wasn't how it was supposed to be. They should have been making love now. And when the sun was a little higher they should have been taking breakfast out there on the terrace, against the backdrop of the most beautiful view in the world. Afterwards, he'd been planning to surprise his new bride with a boat-trip for two along the Amalfi coast, where a sleek yacht lay bobbing in the water—ready to take them to any number of paradise destinations.

And now?

Now it all felt so *empty*.

He turned back to face her, thinking how beautiful she looked, her sapphire eyes glittering wildly in her pale face. He should tell her to get the hell out of his life. To walk out and leave him alone and he would pay her off with a no-fuss divorce.

But the beat of his heart and the heat in his groin were clouding his judgement. Her body was sending out a siren call he'd denied for too long to be strong enough to resist, when it was sitting right there in front of him, on a plate. He began to walk towards the bed and saw her eyes darken as he stood over her, seeing the way that her fingers clutched at the all-enveloping bathrobe.

'What are you doing?' she whispered.

'Nothing, at the moment. Why, what do you want me to do?'

She wanted him to stop looking at her like that—as if she were a piece of *meat* and he were some hungry predator who was about to make a big meal of it. 'I want you to leave me alone.'

'No, you don't.'

'I do, I...*oh*!' Lily fell back against the pillows as he sank down on the bed, his mouth finding hers and prising her lips open with the expert play of his tongue. And she was letting him. Letting his fingers splay over her breast as the robe fell open—and the instinctive cry of pleasure she gave in response to his touch felt like a betrayal. There was still time to struggle. Still time to push him away, even as his hand was reaching for his belt. So why was she *helping* him? Why was she tugging at his trousers and then at the silken boxes which hugged the hard curve of his buttocks? Why the hell didn't she do something as he reached for a condom, which he was now sliding on with a daunting efficiency?

And then he was ripping the shirt from his shoulders and somehow the robe had been pulled from her body. He was prising open her thighs and she was letting him—*wanting him*—so on fire and so wet for him that she sucked in a gasped cry of pleasure as he entered her. For a moment he stilled and then he bent his head to whisper in her ear.

'So why don't you show me what you can do, baby?'

It was an unforgivingly contemptuous remark to make in the circumstances and Lily closed her eyes as she prayed for strength to tell him to stop, knowing that he would comply in an instant. Because hadn't he already demonstrated his steely self-control where sex was concerned? But the truth was that she didn't want him to stop. She couldn't bear him to stop. When he was deep inside her like this, wasn't there the sense that they were at one—only if it was in a purely physical sense?

She placed the flat of her hand on his chest and pushed, until he was lying on his back with her on top, still intimately joined. Her hair fell forward as she began to move, tentatively at first and then, as he gave a shuddered moan, with more confidence. Her soft thighs gripped the hard bone and sinew of his hips. She revelled in the erotic contrast of his taut masculinity against her pliant femininity. She felt the hardness of him deep inside her as she rode him with a hunger and an anger she'd never felt before. And when she saw control begin to slip away from him, she lowered her head and began to kiss him—even though at first he tried to turn his head away. But not for long. With a little moan of capitulation he let her deepen the kiss and he caught his hands to her waist as he came to a shuddering orgasm deep inside her.

She felt the ragged warmth of his breath against her neck as the spasms died away into a soft stillness. For a while, they lay there in silence until he carefully withdrew from her and she felt a great pang of disappointment—hating herself for missing the intimate feel of his body so much.

He turned onto his side, propping himself up on one elbow and leaning over her—his lips very close to hers. 'That was a little one-sided,' he mused.

Lily swallowed. 'It doesn't matter.'

'Oh, but it does.' Slipping his hand down between her thighs, he began to move his fingers against her heated flesh. 'It matters a lot.'

'Ciro—'

'Shh.'

It was quick and it was perfunctory and Lily was much too turned on to be able to stop him from bringing her to another gasping orgasm, which he didn't even bother to silence with a kiss.

Afterwards she felt like turning her face into the pillow and weeping with shame, but she vowed that Ciro would see no tears from her. She had to face the truth—no matter how unpalatable that might be. She couldn't just shrug off all the responsibility and place all the burden on him. If this was a blame-game then there were two players, not one. *She* had helped to create this situation. She'd known the kind of man he was, with his old-fashioned ideals—and she had allowed herself to play along with it. Yes, it had *felt* real to her, but Ciro didn't care about that. He cared about her deception. About the smashing of what he'd believed in—and there was no going back. They needed to confront the future and they needed to do it with dignity.

'So where do we go from here?' she asked slowly.

Ciro looked down at her flushed face and saw the pulse which was beating frantically amid the dampened hair at her temple. Where indeed? He felt the bitter taste of regret, knowing he shouldn't have done that. He shouldn't have had sex with her again—nor brought her to such a cold-blooded orgasm afterwards. He despised himself for his actions—even while his body still shivered with remembered pleasure of how good she'd felt.

For a long moment he was silent as he weighed up all the possibilities which lay open to them. 'If we hadn't consummated the marriage, then we could have had it annulled,' he said. 'As it is, I think we should put an end to it as soon as possible, don't you?'

Lily thought about a pet dog she'd once had—her beloved Harley, who had lived to a ripe old age. When he had become sick the vet had talked about 'putting him out of his misery'. Well, that was exactly what this felt like. Only without the long and happy life in between.

Well, she was damned if she was going to ask him if they couldn't try to work it out—not when he'd clearly made up his mind that it was over.

'I can go back to England,' she said quietly.

Ciro shook his head, his mind working

quickly, the way it always did when he saw a problem which needed a solution. 'No, Lily. That's where you're wrong. I don't want any more drama—and you flouncing out with a haunted face and accusing eyes is the last thing I need. My marriage ending within days will either make me look like a fool—or a bad judge of character. And I will countenance neither.'

'So this is all about *your* reputation, is it, Ciro?'

'What do you think?' he questioned roughly. 'I have worked hard to build it and I will not have it wrecked by you.' He paused, his heart beating heavily as he looked at her. 'If you agree to my plan, then you'll get what you wanted all along. The Grange will still be yours and I will ensure a generous settlement in return for your cooperation.'

Lily heard the steely note of negotiation which had entered his voice and stared at him. He looked like a *stranger*, she thought. A dark-faced and grim stranger. 'What do you mean by cooperation?'

He shrugged. 'It isn't complicated. You play the part of my beloved wife for six months—after which time we will tell the world that you are homesick. That you miss England too much to make the marriage work and that we are parting amicably.'

'And if I refuse?'

'I don't think you will.' His black eyes hardened and so did his lips. 'You see, you aren't really in any position to refuse, Lily.'

She opened her mouth to contradict him, to tell him that she could refuse anything she pleased. But the truth was that she was filled with a weariness which seemed to have seeped deep into her bones. And that, right now, she couldn't face going back to the tatters of the life she'd left behind in England.

CHAPTER TEN

'YOU were very quiet tonight.'

Ciro's words broke into the silence of Lily's thoughts and a whisper of awareness shivered over her skin as he joined her on the balcony. Suddenly the terrace of their apartment seemed the size of a matchbox as he dominated the space around him, just as he always did. The glitter of the starry sky, the dark lick of the waves in the bay— all these seemed to fade into nothingness as he came to stand beside her. She could sense the warmth of his body and smell the raw tang of his aftershave. And it didn't seem to matter how much she tried to fight her attraction towards him, or how often she told herself that it was dangerous to still feel this way about him—nothing ever changed. She continued to want her husband with a fierce hunger which had shown no signs of abating.

They had arrived home a short while ago and she'd gone outside into the warm night air to drink in the view she had grown to love. The magic of the southern city which had captured her heart these last few months—a heart for which her husband had no use.

'You didn't enjoy the evening?' he questioned.

Lily felt the faint whisper of the sea breeze on her bare shoulders and swallowed down a painful sigh. Did he really have no idea why she was so preoccupied? Didn't he realise that no matter how wonderful the opera or after-show party, or whatever other glitzy event they happened to be attending, it didn't make up for the tense reality of their married life. That every second spent beneath his unforgiving gaze was like having a knife twisted in her stomach.

It isn't complicated, Ciro had said on their wedding night—when he had proposed the idea of a six-month marriage for the sake of propriety.

Like hell it wasn't.

It was about as complicated as it could get.

She stared at the diamond sparkle of the sea and the brooding silhouette of Mount Vesuvius in the distance. Did he really find it *uncomplicated* to maintain the illusion that they were a pair of blissful newlyweds, when nothing could be further from the truth?

That was the trouble. Yes, he did. Ciro had a skill which seemed sadly lacking in her. It seemed that he could compartmentalise everything with an ease which would have been almost admirable if it hadn't been so breathtakingly cold. And he could do it so well that at times she'd almost been sucked into believing it herself. Like when he introduced her to people she hadn't met before and his hand would stray to rest protectively at the small of her back—as if he were finding it difficult to refrain from touching her. And Lily's heart would crash like crazy as his fingers massaged the knotted tension in her spine, wondering if he'd forgiven her. But then she would look up into his dark eyes and see nothing but coldness there.

Which either meant that her husband was a brilliant actor who could successfully hide his feelings from the world—or just that he didn't *have* any feelings for her any more. That the supposed 'lightning flash' he'd once felt had been extinguished by her deception.

The morning after their wedding, he had cancelled their honeymoon yacht trip along the Amalfi coastline and Lily had tried telling herself that was a good thing. Because could there be anything worse than being stuck on a boat with a man who was simmeringly angry with you? Yet inside she had been heartbroken—like a child whose birthday party had been called off at the last minute.

So they'd come back to Ciro's apartment and Lily had tried telling herself that surely it couldn't be *that* difficult to maintain their fiction of a relationship—especially as her husband had gone straight back to work instead of taking a planned sabbatical. She was here in Naples, surrounded by beauty and culture and—even if her marriage *was* a disaster—this was an opportunity she'd never have again. She was determined to put a brave face on it. To keep smiling, no matter what. To keep praying that maybe her husband's anger might fade away and that he might let her close enough to love him...

But her prayers went unanswered. The only time he let her close was when he was having sex with her—and she liked *that* far too much to tell him not to do it, no matter how much her battered pride urged her to push him away.

She turned to face him now as the silver moonlight cast indigo shadows on his sculpted features and the sight of him in his dark evening clothes still had the power to make her quiver with lust. 'Of course I enjoyed the evening,' she said. 'The opera was magnificent.'

'I know it was.' There was a pause as he drifted his gaze over her. 'Everyone was commenting on how beautiful you looked.'

She looked up into his dark eyes. 'And what did you say?'

Ciro reached out to frame her cheek with the palm of his hand, feeling the familiar thunder of his pulse. 'Oh, I agreed with them. Because nobody has ever denied your beauty, Lily,' he said softly. 'Least of all me.'

'Ciro—'

But he silenced her breathless whisper with his lips, acknowledging the sweet power of sex to blot out his misgivings, as he pulled her into his arms. Because sometimes when she looked at him with those big blue eyes she made him want to melt. She made him feel almost...*vulnerable*— just as he'd done when he'd made his wedding vows in that music-filled and fragrant church. When he'd felt as if he was poised on the brink of something momentous— only to discover that he was marrying a woman he didn't really know. Who had taken his half-formed dreams and smashed them beneath her perfect little feet until they lay shattered and unrecognisable.

Ciro had been angry with Lily for her deception, yes, he had. But once his anger had died away, he had been almost *grateful* to her. Because it had felt wonderfully familiar to lose himself in the old, familiar coldness—to feel that iciness encase his heart once more. It had put him back in the emotional driving seat, where nothing or no one could touch him. Or hurt him.

In the darkness of the Neapolitan night, he slipped his hand inside the bodice of her dress and heard the rush of her breath as his fingers encountered the silken feel of her bare skin. 'Bed, I think,' he said unsteadily and led her unresisting inside, where he proceeded to strip off her clothes with ruthless efficiency.

His skin was hot against hers and by the time he entered her, she pulled him to her with a fierce hunger, as if she couldn't get enough of him. Her lips sought his and she moaned as he crushed his mouth onto hers, moving inside her body in a way which soon had her shuddering helplessly in his arms. Afterwards she clung to him, her hands clasped behind his neck—only loosening their grip when sleep crept over her and she lolled against the bank of pillows. Deliberately, Ciro rolled over to the other side of the bed—as far from the soft temptation of her body as it was possible to be. He had been doing this more often of late—rationing the time she spent in his arms and telling himself that he needed to get used to solitude again. Because soon his beautiful, duplicitous bride would be heading back to England and he would be left alone…

He slept restlessly, with dreams which left him feeling spooked, and when he awoke, it was to find Lily gone—just like in the dream. For a moment he lay there, staring up at the streaks of sunlight which were dancing across the ceiling—and a terrible sense of darkness invaded his soul.

He showered and dressed, then walked out onto the terrace to find her sitting drinking coffee—her eyes concealed behind her large sunglasses as she automatically bent to pour him a cup. She was wearing a pale, silken robe which had been part of her trousseau and it was easy to see that she was naked underneath.

'So what are you planning to do today?' he asked, a flicker of desire shimmering over him as he began knotting his tie.

From behind the concealment of her shades, Lily watched him. His black hair glittered with tiny drops of water and his skin was still glowing from the shower. He radiated energy and vitality from every pore and, even though he looked cool and businesslike in his lightweight suit, her instinctive feeling was one of pure lust.

Guilt, too. She mustn't forget her ever-present sense of guilt, must she? She remembered the way she'd been last night, in his arms. The way she'd moaned his name out loud as she climaxed—the way she always did. It was all too easy to close her mind to her nagging uncertainties when he was deep inside her like that. She'd just lain right back and enjoyed every second of his love-making and afterwards she had… had…

'Blushing, Lily?' he murmured as he gave his tie one final tug and reached down for his coffee. 'My, my—it's a long time since I've seen you blush.'

She heard the censure in his voice and bristled. 'Perhaps you think only women with intact hymens should be permitted to blush?'

'Isn't that a little crude?' he murmured.

'Which you never are, of course?'

His black eyes glittered. 'You didn't seem

to be complaining about my crudity last night.'

'I doubt whether you've ever had any complaints in that particular department, Ciro.'

Feeling another jerk of desire, he walked over to the edge of the terrace, as if he just wanted to get a better look at the bay. It was a view he'd grown up with and yet which now seemed subtly altered—as everything familiar in his life had been altered.

Had he thought that this charade of a marriage would be easy? That he would pleasure himself with Lily for six, short months and that each time he did he would find himself growing a little more distant from her? Yes, he had. Of course he had. Because that was what he had *wanted* to happen and Ciro was a man who always made things happen.

He had expected his anger to remain constant, while his passion declined—the way it always did when a relationship with a woman was on the wane. The only trouble was that it hadn't worked out like that. A welcome immunity towards her simply hadn't happened and he was no closer to feeling indifferent towards her. In bed and out, he wanted her now as much as he'd always wanted her.

It perplexed him. It was driving him crazy. He told himself over and over that she was a liar who had been prepared to lie in order to secure her future. That she would never understand what made a traditionally Neapolitan man like himself tick. But none of his convictions seemed to last beyond a minute and that confused the hell out of him. What did she *have* that made him instantly want to lose himself in her— as if she alone possessed the balm which could soothe his troubled spirit? Had she cast some kind of spell on him, the moment she'd entered his life?

'Ciro?'

'What?' he growled, turning back to face her, letting his eyes drift over the spill of her hair, which was cascading all the way down her back and wondering whether he should postpone his first meeting and take her back to bed.

'You asked what I was planning to do today.'

'Did I?'

She gave a tight smile but secretly she was rather relieved by his air of distraction, knowing he wasn't going to like what she had to say. 'I thought I'd go and see your mother.'

This piece of information wiped all the confused thoughts from his head and had him frowning as he looked at her. 'Why would you want to do that?'

'Because she's your mother. And I'm your wife.'

'But you're not *really* my wife, are you, Lily? We both know that.'

'I may not be your wife in the true sense of the word—but your mother doesn't know that, does she? And if you want to maintain this fiction of a marriage, then visiting her seems the right thing to do. Anyway, I'd like to go and see her. I can't keep spending every day exploring churches and listening to Italian lessons on my headset while you go out and make yet another fortune.'

She saw his eyes narrow and knew he was still bemused by her insistence on learning a language which wasn't going to be of any use to her in the future. She'd argued with him over this—saying that no new language would ever be wasted. He seemed to think that now she had access to his bank account, she'd want to spend all her days spending it. But Lily hadn't done that—something which she knew perplexed him. She had fallen in love with Naples, and pride made her want to make herself understood while she was living there. For a few brief months, she wanted to feel part of this warm, southern paradise.

Ciro mulled over this latest surprising development. 'My mother isn't a great socialiser,' he said repressively. 'I doubt whether she'll agree to see you.'

'She already has.'

'Scusi?' He stared at her in disbelief.

'I rang her yesterday and said I'd like to go round and she's invited me for coffee.'

Ciro felt the slow build of anger though he couldn't quite pinpoint the cause of it. Because she hadn't checked with him first? Or because he felt uncomfortable about her seeing a woman with whom he'd always had a difficult relationship? 'You went behind my back and phoned my mother and arranged to meet her?'

'Yes, Ciro—if that's how you want to

look at it, I did. I committed the heinous crime of trying to be polite—something which is obviously beyond your comprehension.'

'There's no need to be insolent.'

'Why, have you taken out a monopoly on insolence?' she challenged.

Their eyes met in a silent tussle of wills and for one brief moment Ciro almost smiled. But any humour was dissolved by what she'd just told him. *Why was she starting up a pointless relationship with his mother?*

'Is there nothing I can say which will change your mind?'

'Absolutely nothing. Short of you getting hold of some chains and imprisoning me in the apartment, I'm going round there for coffee this morning.'

'Then so be it.' He picked up his briefcase and his mouth hardened. 'But she can be a difficult woman. Don't say I didn't warn you.'

His words still ringing in her ears, she got ready for her meeting with her mother-in-law, changing her outfit three times and ending up feeling hot and flustered. A taxi took her to Leonora D'Angelo's large apartment and when she was shown into the dimly lit salon she felt big and clumsy compared to the bird-like frame of Ciro's mother.

Lily perched on the edge of a velvet chair and accepted a tiny cup of coffee and a wave of sadness washed over her. How long had it been since she'd sat and drunk coffee with her own mother like this? She wondered what advice she would have given her about Ciro, and realised how much she still missed her.

Despite her advanced years, Leonora D'Angelo remained a handsome woman, with dark eyes so reminiscent of her son and a bone structure which emphasised her angular jaw. She wore a plain grey dress and a twisted gold necklace and on her bony fingers glittered an impressive array of diamonds. She leaned back in her chair and gave Lily a cool smile.

'So. The younger Signora D'Angelo is looking a little pale. You are settling well into Naples, I hope?'

Lily managed to produce a smile, wondering what her mother-in-law would say if she came out and told it how it really was. *I'm just about managing to tolerate living with a man who despises me, even though the feeling isn't exactly mutual. Because learning to unlove someone isn't as easy as you might think.* 'It's a beautiful city,' she said politely.

Leonora nodded. 'I think so—though, to many, Naples is an enigma. A place of light and dark. Where sometimes you turn a corner and never quite know what you'll find.' She gave a thin smile. 'Perhaps a little like my son.'

Lily's heart began to pound as she wondered if Leonora was going to talk about Ciro—because would she be able to sustain the lie of their marriage to a woman who knew him better than anyone? 'Really?' she said, because she couldn't think what else to say.

'I am pleased that Ciro has decided to settle down at last. It has certainly been a long time coming. Sometimes I wonder why that should have been, but there again…' There was a pause as Leonora's voice tailed off and she narrowed her fading dark eyes. 'Does he talk much about his childhood?'

Lily shook her head. 'Not really.'

'He hasn't told you that he was unhappy?'

At this, Lily felt a little helpless. It wasn't really her place to disclose things he'd said to her in confidence. Disclosures which could be potentially very hurtful to his mother. The things Ciro had said were half-admissions which didn't make up a complete picture—like pieces of a jigsaw puzzle with the edges missing. She'd managed to discover that he was often left to fend for himself—and that, despite the army of servants, he'd been a lonely little boy. And how could she possibly turn around to Leonora D'Angelo and tell her that he had also hinted about his mother's love-life and that he heartily disapproved of it?

'Ciro is a very private man,' Lily said, hoping that would be an end to it, but it seemed that was not to be the case because Signora D'Angelo put her untouched coffee down on a highly polished table.

'I was very depressed after I gave birth to him, you know.' Leonora's cultured voice gave an unexpected crack.

'No,' said Lily quietly. 'I didn't know.'

'There was no understanding of the condition back then, of course—and people certainly never spoke of it, because depression has always carried its own kind of stigma. It was expected that a woman should just carry on and it would all work out. And I tried to make that happen, I really did—but my mood was too dark to be lifted.' There was a pause. 'Did you know that his father left me?'

Uncomfortably, Lily nodded. 'He did mention that.'

Leonora shrugged as if it didn't matter and Lily thought that she almost carried it off—but not quite. And suddenly she got a frightening image of herself in some lonely future, shrugging her shoulders and explaining that her Neapolitan marriage hadn't worked out, with a voice like Leonora's—which wasn't quite steady.

'The marriage was not what he thought it would be. He had married a vivacious socialite,' said Leonora. 'Not a woman who could hardly be bothered to get out of bed in the morning. It was highly unusual for a man to leave his wife and child

in those days and after he'd gone, I was...
afraid. Yes, afraid. Frightened of being on
my own. Of having sole charge of a boy as
strong and as wilful as Ciro with no father
figure to look up to. And ashamed of having been rejected. I wanted a man for my
son—and, yes, I admit, I wanted a man
for *me*.'

'Signora D'Angelo,' interrupted Lily
quickly. 'You don't have to tell me all this.'

'Oh, but I do,' said the older woman, her
voice a little bitter now. 'Because maybe
you might be able to explain to Ciro why
I did what I did. To make him listen in a
way that he refuses to do with me.'

Lily bit her lip. If she told the truth—that
Ciro wouldn't dream of listening to a word
she said—then wouldn't that just worry her
mother-in-law even more? She gave a weak
smile. 'I can try.'

Leonora clasped her fingers together in
her lap and her diamonds glittered. 'Things
were different for women then—especially
here. Naples has always been one of the
most traditional and male-centred of cit-
ies. It was frowned on to be a deserted
wife—especially as everyone else I knew

had a husband at home. Maybe I was desperate and don't they always say that desperation shows?' She gave a wry kind of laugh. 'Maybe that was why I never married again, although I used to date men, of course. I used to bring them back here—'

'Signora D'Angelo—'

'Sometimes just for drinks, or for coffee. Sometimes—not always—just to talk. I was *lonely*, Lily. Very lonely.'

Lily nodded as she saw the stark pain in Leonora's eyes. 'Yes, I can imagine,' she said quietly.

'But Ciro was fierce, even then. He hated it. He hated the men. He wanted his mamma to live like a nun and I wanted to live like...well, like a woman.' Leonora swallowed. 'It made us grow apart. It drove a wedge between us and that is something I bitterly regret. And nothing I have said or done since has softened his stance towards me because he has refused ever to discuss it.'

Lily felt a terrible sadness overwhelm her because she could see the problem from Leonora's point of view, as well as from Ciro's. She could imagine the little boy wanting to protect his mother from the men he resented—too young to realise that she needed something other than the love of her child to sustain her. Leonora had wanted to find a man whom Ciro could look up to but had never managed it—and it must have seemed to him like a constant stream of strangers entering his home. Barriers had sprung up between mother and son and time had only made them more impenetrable.

Suddenly, it made it more understandable why Ciro had reacted so badly to the discovery that she wasn't a virgin. Had emotion overcome reason, to make him believe that his supposedly innocent wife would one day take up with other men, as his own mother had done? Or had he simply decided that her lack of innocence equalled a predatory nature? He was a man who saw things in black or white—even women. Especially women. Madonna or Whore. Lots of men thought that way, didn't they? And it wasn't difficult to see which category he had placed her in.

'Won't you talk to him, Lily?' said Leonora

suddenly. 'Won't you try to explain to him what it was like for me?'

Lily heard the faint tremor in her mother-in-law's voice and saw what lay beneath the sophisticated veneer: a frightened woman who was afraid of growing old and dying without the forgiveness of her only child.

'I can try,' she said, knowing that she would give it her very best shot. Because what did she have to lose? Even if Ciro was angry with her for interfering, it wasn't going to change anything between *them*, was it? She was leaving him—and Naples—that had already been decided. Yet if she could leave knowing that she had helped reconcile mother and son—then wouldn't something good have come out of all this mess?

Leonora's disclosure had the effect of making Lily feel as if she'd woken up from an anaesthetic. Of making her want to re-discover something of herself. She realised she had stopped being the Lily who loved to create a cosy nest around her. She'd been so busy trying to *survive* in this hostile atmosphere that she'd completely forgotten who she really was. Yet hadn't Ciro fallen for the woman who had baked cakes and tried to create a warm home? Even if he was still angry about her lack of innocence, surely she could remind him of the woman she had once been and all that she had represented to him.

Suddenly, she could understand his refusal to look beyond the boundaries he had created for himself. She suspected that it was a defence mechanism—to stop himself from being hurt again, the way he'd been hurt as a child. He was a strong man who hated showing vulnerability, but couldn't she convince him that she would never willingly hurt him—not ever again? That if he could forgive her past mistake, then she would gladly open up her heart and love him with every fibre of her being? That she would be loyal and true to him in every way she could.

Filled with sudden hope, Lily found the nearest shop to their apartment. It was a small, dark place with an ancient fan which cut inefficiently through the warm, heavy air. Outside were boxes of oranges and tomatoes and inside were bottles of wine and rows of sweet biscuits. It took her a while to find what she was looking for, but eventually Lily managed to cobble together the ingredients for a cake, much to the surprise of the old woman who served her. Maybe she found it strange that the fair foreigner who spoke such faltering Italian should be baking a cake.

Back at the apartment, she set to work, finding a roasting tray which would serve as a cake tin while seriously wondering whether Ciro's state-of-the-art cooker had ever been used before now. But it felt good to lose herself in the familiar rhythms of baking. To hear the slop of the eggs as they fell onto the flour with a little puff, like smoke. She listened to the beating of the wooden spoon, which her cookery teacher had always said sounded like horses clip-clopping over cobblestones. She grated zest from the juiciest lemons she had ever used and soon the incomparable smell of fresh cake was filling Ciro's very masculine apartment.

She heard the front door slam soon after six. Heard him dropping his suitcase onto the floor and the momentary silence before his footsteps headed towards the kitchen.

His face registered very little when he saw her, save for a barely perceptible narrowing of his eyes. Perhaps he was noticing the inevitable smears of cake-mix on her cotton dress since, naturally, she had no apron here.

'What are you doing?' he questioned slowly.

'You mean apart from making a cake?' she enquired, determinedly cheerful as she opened the smoked glass door of the oven to extract it.

Ciro watched the curve of her bottom as she bent forward and it mimicked the very first time he'd seen her baking, when he'd been blown away by the sight of her luscious young body. The memory should have filled him with desire but instead all he felt was a crushing sense of sadness. He stared at the cake as she put it down. 'What's all this in aid of?'

Would she sound crazy if she told him that she'd needed to reclaim something familiar? Something which would make her feel like herself again—instead of a woman who was just playing a part. She lifted her

eyes to meet his, praying for his understanding.

'I've just realised how long it is since I've
done any baking. Would you like some? It
always tastes best when you eat it straight
from the oven.'

He shook his head as her words seem
to fly out of the air to mock him. She'd
said them once before, a long time ago—
and they reminded him of everything he'd
hoped for. All those simple pleasures which
now seemed a world away from the bit-
tersweet reality of their life together. 'No,
thanks,' he said, wondering why he should
care that her face had crumpled with disappointment and that she was biting on her
lip as if she was trying to stop it from trembling. 'Did you go and see my mother?'

'I did.'

'And?'

Lily stared at him. Maybe if he'd been
a little more understanding—a little
kinder—then she might have trodden carefully. If he'd accepted a slice of warm cake
as a gesture of conciliation, then inevita-
bly she would have softened. But in that
moment his cold face seemed to confirm

all the things his mother had said about him and any thoughts of diplomacy rushed straight out of her mind. 'She told me a few very interesting things.'

Ciro loosened his tie. He wanted to affect lack of interest, to tell her that he didn't really care, but the truth of it was that his curiosity had been aroused. 'Oh?' he questioned. 'Such as?'

She sucked in a deep breath. 'Such as you've never forgiven her for having boyfriends when you were young.'

There was brief, disbelieving pause. 'She said *what*?' he questioned dangerously.

'Did you know that your mother suffered post-natal depression?' she asked quickly. 'And that was one of the reasons your father left her?'

'So it was all his fault?' he snapped.

'It's nobody's *fault*!' she retorted, but she could feel her heart pounding against her ribcage. 'It's just the way things were. Nobody was doing very much about post-natal depression back then. Your mother told me...well, she said she wanted you to have a father figure you could look up to.'

'That was very *good* of her,' he ground

out. 'She certainly auditioned enough men for that particular role!'

'You're hateful,' Lily whispered as she saw the unforgiving hardness in his eyes. 'Can't you see that your mother's getting older and she's terrified she's going to die and that none of this *stuff* will be resolved?'

'That's enough!' he snapped.

'No, it's not,' she fired back. 'It's not nearly enough! I actually found myself feeling sorry for her, for having to put up with your coldness and your control-freakery ways all these years. Except that now I discover that I'm doing exactly the same. I'm behaving in a way I'm growing to despise.'

His voice was a hiss of deadly silk. 'What the hell are you talking about?'

'I'm talking about me accepting the unacceptable! About us maintaining this façade of a marriage for however many months you think we should—just for the sake of your damned *image*!'

There was a pause. 'But we agreed, Lily.'

'Yes, we did,' she said. But hadn't there been an ulterior motive behind her easy agreement, even if she hadn't acknowledged it at the time? Hadn't part of her hoped that time might dissolve some of his anger towards her? That they could get back some of what they'd once had— something which she had called love and which she'd hoped Ciro might one day come to feel for her, too. Except that they hadn't, had they? He had shown no sign of softening—not to the woman who had given birth to him, and not to the woman he'd married either. No matter what their supposed 'sins' were, there was no forgiveness in Ciro D'Angelo's heart for the women who had hurt him. And the longer she stayed, the more damaged her own heart would become. Especially as she just couldn't seem to stop loving him, no matter what he threw at her.

'But I've changed my mind,' she said slowly. 'I can't maintain this false life with you any longer. And I want to go back to England.'

'You can't do that,' he said repressively.

'Why, won't you allow me to?' Fearlessly now, she met his dark eyes. 'Will you go one step further in your very convincing role as tyrant husband and try to stop me?

Chain me to the sofa, perhaps—or keep me on a very long leash?'

She didn't wait for him to answer, just ran to the bathroom and locked the slammed door behind her. She stared at her ashen face in the mirror and heard the loud beat of her heart, knowing there was one certain way guaranteed to give her back her freedom. But could she do it? Could she go through with it?

She was in there for ten minutes before she heard him calling her name and knew she had to face him—because wasn't that the whole point of what she'd done? But the taste in her mouth was bitter as she slowly opened the door to him and she saw the revulsion in his eyes even before she heard the ragged breath of horror he sucked in.

'Per l'amor del cielo!' he exclaimed harshly. 'Lily, what have you done?'

She saw his disbelieving gaze travelling over her shoulder, where thick strands of her hair were lying all over the bathroom floor, like shiny heaps of harvested corn. Together with an unfamiliar lightness of head, she felt the jagged, shorn locks brushing against her jaw and she raised it up towards him in a defiant gesture.

'What have I done? I've broken my promise,' she said, unable to keep the emotional tremor from her voice, because that revulsion was still on his face. And for the first time ever, she recoiled from the hand that reached out and touched her. For once, the feel of his fingers on her arms did not trigger off an unstoppable lust but a sensation of disgust. How could she have let herself stay in such a terrible situation? Giving herself night after night to a man who clearly despised her. Did she have no pride; no self-respect?

She pulled away from him, her breath coming short and fast from her throat. 'I've cut my hair!' she declared. 'It's something I said I wouldn't do but now I have. I've broken my promise and it's symbolic and final. I'm freeing you from our marriage, Ciro—and I'm freeing myself, too. And I want…no, I *need* to go home.'

CHAPTER ELEVEN

HE DIDN'T try to stop her. That was the part which shattered Lily most of all. Ciro didn't say a word to try to change her mind about leaving. Yet when she stopped to think about it—had she really expected anything different? Had she imagined that her proud and unforgiving husband would turn round and beg her to stay? To maintain this farce of a marriage?

In fact she was taken aback by the speed of his reaction to her demand to go home. It was as if he'd suddenly realised that the kind of woman who hacked off her hair in a moment of high emotion would never have made a suitable wife for a high-born Neapolitan. His face looked as if it had been sculpted from a hard, dark marble as he looked at her.

'Perhaps this is all for the best,' he said,

in an odd, flat voice. 'When do you want to leave?'

'As soon as possible!' she blurted out, knowing that to prolong this state of affairs would be an agony which would only add to her growing heartache. 'I'll fly out this afternoon, if I can.'

His horrified gaze returned to the piles of silken hair which were still lying on the bathroom floor and then he lifted reluctant eyes to the shorn strands which untidily framed her face. 'Wouldn't you rather go and see a hairdresser first?'

His question only added to her distress, even though she suspected he might have a point. Because didn't the hasty cut give her the appearance of some crazy woman, who would bring disrepute to the D'Angelo name?

She shook her head. 'I'll cover it up with a hat.' Her voice rose to a note of near-hysteria. 'Who knows? It might start a new trend of do-it-yourself hairdressing.'

Ciro felt the twisting of some nameless emotion as he looked at her, thinking that the short style made her face seem all eyes.

Enormous sapphire eyes which were glittering up at him with the suspicion of tears.

'I'll have my lawyers draw up a contract—and the Grange will be signed over to you as part of the divorce settlement. I will also honour my commitment to pay your brother through his course at art school.' He gave a bitter laugh. 'You might as well leave the marriage with what you came into it for. Riches beyond your wildest dreams, wasn't it, Lily?'

The accusation hit her hard and Lily sucked in an unsteady breath, feeling slightly ill as she realised that he'd written her off as mercenary. 'I don't want anything from you, Ciro.'

'You want the Grange.'

Fighting back tears, she shook her head. 'I don't want it that much.' Because wouldn't her old family home feel *tainted* if she accepted it under such dreadful circumstances? Wouldn't *she* feel tainted if she came over as greedy and grasping? And she was damned if she was going to give Ciro yet another reason to despise her.

'You want your brother to go to art school.'

'Not at any price. We'll work it out somehow. If Jonny is good enough, then he'll get a scholarship. And if he's not—well, something else will come his way, because that's how life works for most people.'

'Proud words, Lily—but I doubt whether you mean them.' His mouth gave a twist. 'You'll soon change your mind when you speak to my lawyers. I always find there's something very persuasive about seeing hard offers of cash written down in black and white.'

'But that's where you're wrong, Ciro,' she returned, the cynicism of his words sending an icy shiver down her spine. 'When will you get it into your head that this was never about the money?'

'Then what was it about?' Dark eyebrows arched with arrogant disbelief. 'The thunderbolt?'

She wanted to say yes. To tell him that what he'd felt about her had been mutual—but what would be the point when he'd never believe her? Ciro had fallen for someone who didn't really exist—a make-believe woman he'd put on some unachievable pedestal. And maybe she'd fallen for someone who didn't exist, too. Because no matter how powerful his passion for her, there was no way that he was ever going to make a good husband. What kind of future could ever be found with a man who was always so coldly judgemental about women?

'It doesn't matter any more,' she said, in a small voice. 'It's over.'

Ciro flinched as her words filled him with unexpected pain, but he told himself she was right. It *was* over. And maybe her abrupt departure would be best—for both of them.

He made a couple of telephone calls and two hours later he was carrying her bags downstairs, where a driver was waiting to take her to the airport. The last thing he remembered seeing was the glitter in her bright blue eyes, before she quickly put on a large pair of shades. Then she tugged at the floppy straw hat which concealed the unfamiliar hairstyle and, almost impulsively, stood on tiptoe to brush her lips over his cheek.

'Goodbye, Ciro,' she said, in a strange, gulping kind of voice. 'You…you take care of yourself.'

'You, too,' he said—but a sudden sense of something almost like *panic* unsettled him. As if he'd just jumped out of an aircraft and forgotten to put on his parachute. 'Lily—'

'Please. Let's not drag this out any more than we need to,' she said quickly as she moved away from him and climbed into the car.

He watched as she was driven away, waiting for her to turn back to look at him one more time—but she didn't. All he could see was the stiff set of her shoulders and the large hat which hid her shorn head from the world. For a moment he stood completely still, oblivious to the people who passed him by. And when eventually he went back inside, he was surprised to find that his heart was still heavy, though he reassured himself that such a reaction was only natural after such an unexpectedly emotional departure. And that within a few days the memory of his brief marriage would fade.

But it didn't happen that way. The reality was very different—and it took Ciro by surprise. He found that his life had changed in so many ways. It had changed by her coming here, as well as by her leaving. And it was the little things which seemed to mock him most and to remind him that she really had gone. Suddenly, the bed seemed too big. He would wake in the mornings, his hand groping towards the space beside him, to find nothing but emptiness and an unruffled sheet instead of Lily's soft and welcoming body.

He soon discovered that, once word got round that his wife had gone back to England, he was being seen as being 'back on the market', with a corresponding flurry of interest from the opposite sex. And he didn't like it. He didn't like it one bit. The women who came onto him repulsed him and he found their conversation dull. He realised that Lily had been excellent company on their many evenings out—as well as having many other obvious attractions once they'd returned home. Dinner suddenly seemed either a too-solitary meal, or a ritual to be endured amid company he had no wish to join.

He phoned the London office of his lawyers, wanting to hear that she had grasped the very generous settlement he was offering her—as if hearing that would remind himself of her mercenary nature. But she had done no such thing. Slowly, Ciro registered what the bemused voice of his lawyer was telling him. That Lily D'Angelo was walking away from the marriage with nothing.

'Nothing?' Ciro echoed in disbelief.

'Niente,' came the answer in Italian, just so there could be no misunderstanding.

Ciro brooded. He asked someone he knew in London to investigate what she was doing and the answer which came back surprised him. She was still living in the apartment above the tearoom and had resumed her job as a waitress. She had gone back to Chadwick Green. It perplexed him to think she had settled for so little when she could have had so much—and it threw all his certainties into doubt. Until some news came to him from the same investigator, which he regarded with a grim kind of satisfaction.

She had put her mother's pearls up for auction!

Ciro felt a resigned satisfaction as he read that the beautiful necklace had exceeded its reserve price many times over. The necklace which had reminded her of her dead mother had been sold to a mystery buyer in America. So much for sentiment! He remembered the way her blue eyes had clouded over when she'd told him that her stepmother had taken them. And her touching gratitude as he'd recovered them and placed them around her neck. He'd imagined that she had been thinking of her mother at the time, when the truth was far more materialistic. She had realised, of course, the enormous value of the jewels—and known that they would always provide her with a sizeable little nest-egg until she found herself some other poor sucker to support her.

Ciro threw himself into work in an attempt to get her out of his mind, but that very same week brought a postcard from England. It was from Lily's brother—an odd composition of clashing colours which he'd clearly painted himself. The message on it was brief.

Hi, Ciro. Got thumbs-up from art school this a.m. due to exam results.

Start September. Just wanted to thank you (or perhaps I should say mille grazie!*) for making it all possible. See you soon, Jonny.*

Ciro stared at the card in confusion. The sentiment expressed seemed to suggest that Jonny had no idea his sister and her new husband had parted. More than that, he also seemed to be under the illusion that Ciro had financed his art-school funding. What the hell was going on?

He walked out onto the terrace, his heart beating very fast as he tried to piece it all together. Until he realised that there was only one possible source for the funding—and all the implications which came from that. He bunched his hands into two tight fists which hung by the sides of his tensed thighs. *Had Lily sold her mother's precious pearls to put her brother through school?* Had he misjudged her all along?

He stared out at the dark blue blur of the bay but he could see nothing except the glitter of his wife's eyes as she said goodbye to him. He felt a terrible regret wash over him. What had he *done*?

He stood there as the sun sank into the water, until the terrace was lit only by the silver light of the rising moon. Was it too late to go to her and ask for a forgiveness he did not deserve? One which his proud and defiant Lily would probably not give. His mouth hardened as he went back inside to get his passport. Maybe it was too late, but he knew he had to try.

But first there was something he needed to do.

CHAPTER TWELVE

THE windows weren't dirty by any stretch of the imagination, but Lily was still determined to give them a polish. Danielle had repeatedly teased her and said that these days she was nothing but a 'clean freak' and Lily hadn't bothered to deny what was essentially the truth. Because she *did* find housework oddly soothing. It didn't demand too much and it helped make her little apartment look as good as possible. She would listen to the radio, her thoughts easily distracted by the phone-in conversations. And listening to other people talking was much easier than having to talk herself. When people asked *her* questions these days, she didn't know how to answer. But there was no point worrying about it. It was still early days after the break-up of her marriage and she was still trying to settle back into her old life.

Her old life which had become her new life.

She'd been back in Chadwick Green for almost a month now and, in many ways, it was almost as if nothing had changed. The tearoom was still there and so was her little apartment. And her friends. A concerned Fiona had told her that of course she could have her old job back, and Danielle had been overjoyed to see her. But of course, they were worried about her—even though they did their best to hide it. The sight of her radical haircut had visibly shocked them—as had her unmistakable weight-loss.

Danielle had come right out and asked her what had happened in Naples and Lily had been tempted to offload some of her terrible heartache. But how could she possibly explain the convoluted chain of events which had led to her return? She thought about Ciro. She thought about him nearly all the time. About all the hopes he'd had for their future—hopes which she had shared. About each of them wanting to build something strong and permanent: a unit which would last. But look at how they had failed. She'd been so quick to condemn him for his old-fashioned immovability on the subject of her virginity. She had been so frustrated by his inability to adapt to what was, rather than what he wanted it to be. She could see that in a way it had been a *relief* for him to think that she was some kind of gold-digger and predator, like the other women he'd known.

Yet she had deliberately kept her sexual history a secret, hadn't she? She couldn't deny that. She'd done it because she'd wanted to hang onto the dream he'd been offering her. She had allowed herself to paint a false image of reality, to pretend it was the way she'd *wanted* it to be. It didn't matter what her motives had been—that had been wrong. So it followed that she had an equal part to play in the breakdown of their marriage. Their brief love and the subsequent fall-out was intensely private. She would not blacken her husband's name—not to anyone. How could she, when she still loved him?

Outside, the weather had been sunny and

golden. It had been one of the best English summers on record and there had been times when Lily wished it had been otherwise. Wouldn't it have reflected her mood if they'd had the usual downpours of rain, or a spot of unseasonal cold which meant you were tempted to put the heating on? As it was, she had no desire to go out and get some sun on her pale skin—or to join Danielle on a train trip down to the coast. It was bad enough having to listen to the loud revelry of the drinkers who were currently cluttering up the front of the pub next door.

Determined to make the windows look diamond-bright, she filled a bowl with hot water and placed it on the window sill, aware of how bare her neck felt without the tickle of a long strand of hair which occasionally used to tumble down. Her shorn hairstyle still took some getting used to and it made her smile when people who knew her did a double take when they first saw it. She'd been to the nearest big town and put herself in the hands of a hairdresser recommended by Danielle, emerging with her corn-coloured hair shaped close to her head and feathered around her face. After the initial shock, she was beginning to like it. It made her look different, yes—but maybe that was a good thing. She *was* different and there was no denying that. She'd been through a big, painful experience and something like that always changed people.

She cleaned and polished the windows, then opened them wide to let in some fresh air. Cars slid past on the road outside and as she listened to the rising laughter of drinkers outside The Duchess of Cambridge she wondered if she would always feel this way. Would she ever feel like part of the real world again, instead of someone who didn't fit in? Or was she doomed to be one of those shadowy figures who always sat on the sidelines, for ever mourning their lost love?

She was just about to go and make some tea when her attention was caught by the sight of someone walking across the village green towards her. She blinked. An instantly recognisable man with jet-dark hair and a towering physique. He was wearing a snowy shirt and some fine grey trousers and the similarity to the first time she'd ever seen him was so marked that her heart clenched painfully in her chest.

Ciro!

Ciro?

She gripped the window sill for support, sucking in a ragged breath. Because it hurt to see him. It hurt because it reminded her of what she could have had. And because she still loved him.

His powerful stride quickly brought him beneath her window where he stopped and looked up to see her framed there and their eyes met in a long moment. She drank in the sight of him—the angled slant of his cheekbones and the thick lashes which made his dark eyes look so smoulder-ingly sexy. His hair gleamed like tar in the bright sunlight and his olive skin had a soft, golden glow. But his expression was grim as he nodded his head in greeting, like someone giving themselves a silent pep talk.

Lily was aware that the sound of the drinkers had died away and it seemed as if the whole world were silent and holding its breath, save for the birdsong which twit-tered through the air. She leaned forward, her heart pounding so loudly she was certain he must be able to hear it. She opened her mouth to speak, trying to keep the quaver from her voice—to make herself sound stronger than she actually felt. Because she hoped she'd got through the worst of the hurt and she didn't think she could bear to go through it all again. 'What are you doing here?'

'No ideas, Lily?'

'The tearoom's shut,' she said flippantly.

'I don't give a damn about the tearoom. I've come to see you.'

She sucked in another breath. Hadn't they said everything there was to say? Weren't his team of fancy lawyers drawing up the wretched divorce papers even now? 'Why?'

Ciro's eyes narrowed. Her stark question was completely at odds with her delicate appearance and he paused as he studied a face made elfin by her new feathered hairstyle—flinching to think it had been his cruelty which had made her chop off her glorious hair. He'd had a statement planned—whole reams of things he'd intended to say when he saw her. But now all words failed him—except perhaps for the only ones which mattered.

'I've come to say sorry.'

Lily felt dizzy, wondering if she'd imagined those words, but the unusually sombre expression on Ciro's face told her she hadn't. Dimly, she registered that there was still an unusual silence outside the The Duchess of Cambridge and how much the regulars would be loving this. She pulled herself together. 'We can't have this conversation here.'

'Then you'd better come downstairs and let me in.'

Lily's heart raced even though she felt a mild flare of irritation. So he'd lost none of his customary arrogance! But she felt weak as she went downstairs and weaker still when she opened the door and he looked at her with such longing and regret in his dark eyes that her heart turned over. Seeing him this close again made her realise how much she had missed him—in every way it was possible to miss a man. Her instinct was to hurl herself into those strong arms and let him hold her and tell her that everything was going to be okay, but she'd learnt by now that her instincts were often dangerous.

So she stepped aside to let him in, aware of his raw, tangy scent as he passed and re-alising that the small hallway was much too claustrophobic for any kind of conversation. That his compelling proximity might have her doing things she would later regret. And that she needed to put some real space between them. 'You'd better come upstairs.'

Ciro followed her up the narrow stair-way, trying not to be mesmerised by the sway of her bottom and the swish of her cotton dress as she walked. The pulse at his temple was hammering and the inside of his mouth felt like sand. Had he thought that the apology he'd uttered downstairs would be enough and that she would for-give him instantly? Maybe he had. He was not a man known for saying sorry and per-haps he had overestimated its effect on people.

He walked into the sitting room and saw that she had been working hard. New, flower-sprigged curtains hung at the win-dows and she had made some sort of throw which partially disguised the sofa bed. Over the fireplace hung a large and brightly coloured painting whose style he recognised instantly.

'Jonny's?' he asked.

It wasn't what she had been expecting him to say and she turned to him with a slightly puzzled look on her face. 'Yes. How did you know?'

'Because he sent me a postcard. He has a very recognisable technique.'

'Have you come up here to discuss Jonny's artistic merits?'

'Actually, they do have some relevance on what I'm about to say.'

Lily's eyes narrowed. 'Now I'm intrigued.'

'You sold your mother's pearls to pay him through art school, didn't you, Lily?'

Her eyes widened. 'And if I did?'

'Yet you turned down what was rightfully yours.' He lowered his voice as he studied her closely. 'A divorce settlement which meant you could have kept the necklace which meant so much to you.'

She shook her head and in that moment she could have pummelled her fists against him in frustration. 'You just don't get it, do you, Ciro? All your life you've seen things in terms of credit and debit. Everything for you is quantifiable. Everything has to have a *price*!'

'But that's where you're wrong, Lily,' he said, shaking his head. 'I *do* get it. I just wonder why it took me so long. You didn't accept the settlement because you didn't want to be beholden to me in any way.'

'Oh, bravo,' she applauded softly.

'But it's more than that. I suddenly realised that you don't care about *things* as much as you care about people. That the most precious piece of jewellery in the world—even if it did have immense sentimental value—would mean nothing to you if it meant that your brother's dreams were thwarted. So you sold the pearls to put Jonny through art school.'

Lily walked over to the window, but stood with her back to the view. 'How did you find out?'

'That postcard he sent was to thank me for funding his place. I realised then what you must have done.'

'Okay, so now you know. But none of

what you've told me tells me why you're here, Ciro.'

Had he thought that might be enough? That his opening words of apology accompanied by an explanation might be sufficient for her to forgive him? Yes, he had. But he could see now that he had been wrong. That her blue gaze was very steady. He had hurt her badly, he realised—and she was scared he was going to hurt her again.

'Because I'm sorry for having judged you so wrongly,' he said savagely. 'That I was right about you all along—that you aren't like other women. And that there isn't a predatory or mercenary bone in your beautiful body.'

Lily sucked in an unsteady breath. 'Don't—'

'No, wait. I haven't finished.' He suddenly realised why he'd always damned the words 'I love you' as being too easy to say, because in a way—they were. But he also knew how important they were. That they meant so much—and especially to women. But right then, he discovered that they meant a lot to him, too.

'I love you, Lily,' he said simply. 'And my life has been empty without you. I thought I'd be able to go back to the man I'd been before, but I can't and, what's more, I don't want to. *Because I am no longer that man.* You have changed me, Lily. You've changed the way I think. The way I view the world—and other people in it.'

'Ciro—'

'Let me tell you this,' he said urgently. 'After you'd gone, the apartment seemed so…*empty* and I thought about everything you'd said about me and about my unforgiving nature. I sat there for a long time mulling it over and then I went to see my mother—'

She blinked in surprise. 'You did?'

'Yes, I did. For the first time in my life, I listened properly to what she had to say. I tried to see what had happened from an adult point of view, rather than a child's. She asked for my forgiveness and I gave it to her and then I asked for hers, and she reciprocated. And I wept,' he admitted, feeling the lump rise in his throat as he remembered the powerful emotion which had taken him by surprise. 'But I was weeping for my own lost love as much as anything else. Can you believe that, Lily? Ciro D'Angelo shedding tears?'

She nodded. 'Yes, I can—and so what? Tears don't make you less of a man,' she declared fiercely. 'They make you more of a man. Because a man who is afraid of showing his feelings is an emotional coward and you're no coward, Ciro!'

He walked over to the window to where she stood, her face working furiously as she tried to contain her own emotion. And he was staring at her as if it had been a lifetime since he'd seen her rather than a few short weeks. 'My mother told me something I already knew—that you were the best thing that had ever happened to me and I had been a fool to let you go. But how could I have stopped you from going, when I had judged you so harshly? I realised I had to ask for your forgiveness—and to ask whether you'd consider coming back to me.' For a moment he didn't speak, but maybe that had something to do with the difficulty he was having framing these very important words. 'To be my wife again, only this time—my wife in every sense there is. No pretence, Lily. Only honesty. And love. Enduring love.'

Lily bit her trembling lip. Surely he must have read the answer in eyes which were suddenly having to blink back tears of her own? But through her haze of gratitude that he had come to her like this, she realised that she must take her part of the blame. That Ciro should not bear all the burden of what had gone wrong.

'I was wrong not to have told you I wasn't a virgin.'

'It doesn't matter,' he said, feeling like a man who had been walking around half-asleep. How could he have ever thought it important enough to risk losing her?

'I realise that it probably seemed like a deliberate deception, but that's not how I ever intended it to be, Ciro. You see, I loved you so much that it felt like the first time and the only time for me. You made the past fade into something so insignificant, it was almost as if it had never happened.'

'You *loved* me?' he repeated, his eyes narrowing. 'Past tense?'

'I love you—present tense,' she said softly. 'Now and always. My darling Ciro.

The man without whom I feel only half a person.'

For a moment he was too choked to speak. Too full of emotion to do anything but pull her into his arms and to hold her very tightly. At last he lowered his head and kissed her, as he'd dreamed of doing since that bleak day when she'd walked out of his life. When he had pushed her so far that there had been nowhere left for her to go.

But there was no need for her to run any more. No need for him to have to go and find her. From now on they would always be together—either here, or in Naples. Wherever they were didn't matter, just as long as they were together. Because when they were together, any four walls became a place they could call home.

EPILOGUE

CIRO looked at the large canvas. 'What's it supposed to be?'

'Don't be so obtuse, darling,' whispered Lily. 'It's *you*, of course. Jonny's very proud of it—and all his tutors all love it. So you mustn't say anything negative about it over lunch. Promise me.'

Ciro screwed up his eyes to observe a crudely drawn circle containing two black spots and a large splodge of orange, shaped like a carrot. He failed to see any resemblance to himself, indeed to anything at all—except perhaps for a snowman. But if the connoisseurs in the art world applauded it, then who was he to question their judgement?

'I promise you I will give him nothing but the praise he so richly deserves. And since it's helped earn him a distinction and the opportunity to go and study in Paris, then it must be good,' he told Lily diplomatically.

Lily gave a little sigh of pleasure as she thought about Jonny's wonderful degree results, wondering if this much happiness could possibly be good for a person. Sometimes she'd wake up and wonder if she might be dreaming—usually when she got out of bed in the morning and wandered out onto the terrace of their Neapolitan home to stare at the matchless view of the bay. But she was just as likely to wake up with disbelieving pleasure in her old home.

Ciro had decided against turning the Grange into a hotel. Instead, they had lovingly restored it into the beautiful home it was meant to be and which they visited whenever possible. She knew that he intended it should go to Jonny and, indeed, there was plenty of room to provide a huge artist's studio for her talented brother. In fact, there might end up being several studios. Jonny had been speaking to Ciro about the possibility of opening up the house for painters who were financially stretched—as artists so often were. And Ciro had warmly embraced the idea.

She looked up to find his dark eyes smiling at her and she smiled back. 'I'm just going to freshen up before lunch.'

'Then I will wait for you here, *dolcezza*,' he murmured indulgently.

Finding a restroom and running her wrists under the cold tap, Lily stared at herself in the mirror, thinking how much she had changed. And how women's lives were often reflected in their hairstyles. For the first few years of their marriage, she'd kept the style really short. Ciro had insisted he liked it—and she believed him. That declaration meant a lot to her, for all kinds of reasons—though she was no longer the insecure woman who believed he only fancied her when she had cascading hair! People often told her that with her elfin look she reminded them of the actress Mitzi Gaynor, who had also worn the distinctive nineteen fifties clothes which Lily favoured.

But lately, she'd made a few sartorial decisions. For a start, she was letting her hair grow—because it required too much in the way of maintenance. And soon, she wasn't going to have quite so much time for getting her hair cut…

The other thing she'd done was to start buying clothes in more contemporary styles. Money was no longer tight and it was foolish to pretend that it was. She didn't have to make them herself any more—and there were plenty of designs which suited her, since curves seemed to be back in fashion. And besides, what woman wanted to get stuck in a fashion rut? These days, she experimented with sharp, modern looks—and floaty creations in pure silk for more formal functions.

Her fingers drifted to the row of creamy pearls at her neck. Ciro had managed to buy them back—*again*. Though he'd told her with mock severity that this was getting to be a habit and that this time they were keeping them. He'd said that maybe one day they'd have a daughter of their own who would wear them. Lily smiled dreamily at her reflection. Maybe they would.

She went back to where Ciro and her brother were waiting for her. Jonny's hair had grown—it fell almost to his shoulders now and his soulful good looks attracted plenty of attention from the opposite sex. In fact, there was a gorgeous creature hanging onto his arm, wearing a sequinned mini-dress, improbably teamed with a pair of pink wellington boots.

'I thought I'd walk Fleur to the station before lunch,' he said. 'If that's okay, sis?'

'That's absolutely fine,' said Lily. 'Ciro and I will wait for you in the restaurant. It was lovely to have met you, Fleur—and hope you have a great summer.'

'Thanks,' said Fleur, with a smile. 'And you.'

Lily looped her hand through Ciro's arm as they watched the young couple walk away, thinking how curiously *grown-up* she felt today.

'You're very quiet,' he murmured. 'Which usually means trouble. Shall we go to the restaurant and I can buy us a very nice bottle of champagne while you bask in the glory of your clever brother and you can tell me what's on your mind?'

She turned her face up to his, her eyes shining. 'That sounds perfect. Though I don't think I'm going to be drinking any champagne.'

'But we're supposed to be celebrating.'

'And we are,' she whispered. 'But there's more than one cause for celebration. I've got something to tell you. I was going to wait until tonight, until we got home, but I don't think I can wait a minute longer.'

He stared at her with an expression she'd never seen on his face before. 'You're going to have a baby?' he questioned unsteadily.

'Yes.' She nodded her head, her lips clamping together to try to keep back her tears of joy. *Yes!*

For one long moment he did nothing, as if the words were taking time to really sink in. And then Ciro put his arms round her and kissed her. He kissed her so thoroughly that she was giggling as they came up for air. And then he bent his head and kissed her some more.

But fortunately they were in an art gallery, where love was one of the things which kept painters in business. And nobody paid the slightest attention to the man and the woman who stood locked in passionate embrace beneath a brightly coloured canvas.

* * * * *